BOARDINGHOUSE STEW

BOARDINGHOUSE STEW

NEW EDITION

E. E. Smith

PHOENIX INTERNATIONAL, INC.

FAYETTEVILLE

Copyright © 2011 by E. E. Smith

Inquiries should be addressed to:
Phoenix International, Inc.
17762 Summer Rain Road
Fayetteville, Arkansas 72701
Phone (479) 521-2204
www.phoenixbase.com

Library of Congress Cataloging-in-Publication Data

Smith, E. E. (Evelyn Eileen), 1932–
  Bordinghouse stew / E.E. Smith. — New ed.
     p. cm.
  ISBN 978-0-9835615-1-4 (alk. paper)
  1. Smith, E. E. (Evelyn Eileen), 1932—Childhood and youth—
Anecdotes. 2. Sacramento (Calif.)—Social life and customs—20th
century—Anecdotes. 3. World War, 1939-1945—California—
Sacramento—Anecdotes. 4. Boardinghouses—California—
Sacramento—Anecdotes. I. Title.
  F869.S12S64 2011
  979.4'54053—dc23
                                                    2011024982

To Teddy Soberjowski, wherever you are

CONTENTS

PREFACE

The old adage "as unpredictable as boardinghouse stew" has been used to describe a situation where no one can say for certain what will happen next. It was certainly an apt description of America in the early days of World War II.

Boardinghouse Stew is my way of bringing into focus and putting into words and actions those days which now seem so remote and, for some, almost unimaginable.

By 1943, the war had already brought such changes to people's lives, and such disruption to old moral codes and values, that one character in my story observes, prophetically, "We'll never be the same in this country!"

While the nation as a whole grappled with a myriad of new and complex situations brought on by the war, the West Coast was caught up in a unique controversy—the removal of resident Japanese and Japanese-Americans to so-called relocation centers away from the areas where they were alleged to be a threat to national security. Motivated by fear, greed,

Newspaper headlines, "Ouster of All Japs in California Near," 1943.
Library of Congress Collection.

jealousy, and racism, many otherwise rational citizens
—some of them prominent, like Earl Warren—joined
the stampede to "get the Japs out of California."

The story of *Boardinghouse Stew* is set in a seedy,
down-at-heel Sacramento boardinghouse, and involves
a lady I will call Mrs. Mumson, her six paying guests,
and others. I should explain here that few real names

are used in my little historical essay, which is the only thing not entirely factual about it. Being blessed (or cursed!) with a remarkable ability to remember people, events, and even conversations of the past, everything here, except for names, is as true and accurate as I can make it. Although, as I explain later, how six intervening decades might have influenced my own ability to remember is an unknown factor. So, before ever beginning work on this book, I read on microfilm several years of the Sacramento newspapers of that era, besides researching the history of the Japanese in California, in an effort to make events and the language of the day as historically accurate as possible.

This, then, is not a work of fiction, though facts may be mixed with personal observations and conversations to make them more interesting. The great writer W. Somerset Maugham said, "Fact is a poor story-teller," so, for many of his World War I stories, he used mainly fictionalized accounts of his experience as a British Secret Service agent.

But back to California and World War II.

With the evacuation of the Japanese and Japanese-Americans from the area, Mrs. Mumson was left without Yukie, her gardener and houseboy. At the same time, domestic workers were flocking to factories and shipyards for better paying jobs, and her maid in the boardinghouse had joined the stampede. The resulting labor shortage made it almost impossible to find any kind of domestic help. Finally, in desperation, the lady is forced to hire a temporary replacement, a young schoolgirl named Eileen, for the summer.

In addition to her other duties Eileen is the cook. But her strange recipes, inspired by a serious crank in the newspaper calling herself "Miss Kitchen," become a running joke.

Through one crisis after another (some more comic than tragic), and in spite of their many differences, Mrs. Mumson and her paying guests—Teddy, Howard, and Doc, as her "boys," and Iris, Margaret, and Patsy, as her "girls"—manage to pull together and become a kind of family. In the center of it all is Eileen, narrating their stories, which she is able to observe from her unique vantage point behind the swinging kitchen door that never quite closes on its rusty hinges.

—E. E. Smith

BOARDINGHOUSE STEW

CHAPTER ONE

SETTING THE STAGE

Just how many of the stories I have often told about the big old house on a broad, tree-lined street in Sacramento, California, are in fact honest-to-God *true*, and how many came out of a lively childhood imagination, obscured (or enhanced) by six intervening decades, is surely open to question. Somewhere between "honest to God" and "open to question" may be nearer the mark. Some things I know for certain. It was a big old house on a broad, tree-lined street in Sacramento. Moreover, it was not merely a house. Not in 1943, anyway. That year, and perhaps for some years after, it was a boardinghouse. I saw it again not long ago. It had undergone a loving (and no doubt hideously expensive) renovation. It is no longer a boardinghouse, and that seems a shame, really.

Boardinghouses have long since gone out of fashion, but in the 1940s they were quite popular, especially in West Coast cities like Sacramento with booming war industries that attracted thousands of new workers needing instant, safe, affordable housing. They were also, for the most part, respectable. A young woman, even if she could afford it, would think twice about risking her reputation by living alone. A young man might take a room in a boardinghouse while saving enough money to get married.

Besides young people, there were others who benefited from the popularity of the boardinghouse. Older, middle-class women, many of them widowed, often found themselves alone in vast houses after the children were grown. Like it or not (and some didn't), establishing a boardinghouse was sometimes the only way to save their homes and, at the same time, keep themselves out of the poorhouse. One such lady was Mrs. Mumson.

Mumson was not her real name, but a close enough approximation, and may discourage lawsuits by living relatives, if she has any. Not that I think anyone, even a cranky relation, will find what I have to say about the lady I am calling Mrs. Mumson to be truly libelous. And let me hasten to add that in real life she did have many good qualities. Generally she was kind and even motherly toward the six "guests," as she preferred to call them, who lived in her home. (She was adamant that hers was not a boardinghouse, it was a *guest* house.) And whether she was genuinely concerned for their well-being or just plain nosey, she took an active interest in their lives.

On the downside she was, to a maddening degree,

incapable of managing anything—whether you called it a boardinghouse or a *guest* house—without someone to do all the work, not to mention looking after her, too. Which is where I came in. But back to Mrs. Mumson.

Her paralyzing indolence might well have been the result of her upbringing in a wealthy family, somewhere in the south, I think, who lived a life of ease with plenty of servants to "do" for them. And I must say it sounded idyllic. In the oppressive afternoon heat in Sacramento she would often drift into a dreamy reverie about summers at home (wherever it was), with cool breezes coming up over the water, family and friends dressed in white for croquet on the lawn, and maids bringing them iced drinks on silver trays. How she got from there to a sweltering run-down-at-heel boardinghouse in California I was soon to learn.

In 1943 I flatly declared that I would not pick tomatoes again that summer, no matter what. A crippling shortage of workers had growers scrambling to find enough people to pick the crops, and that year our summer vacation had been extended by a full month in order to attract more school kids for the job. But spending another summer picking tomatoes in that blazing Sacramento Valley sun, even for a whopping sixty-five cents an hour, did not appeal to me. I had inherited my sister's old bicycle when she got into high school (and wouldn't be caught *dead* riding a bike), but I longed for one of my own. You would have to wait until after the war was over to get a new one, of course, but sometimes you could find a good used bike for sale through the newspaper. They were not cheap—the one I eventually bought cost forty dollars, which was a lot of money in 1943—and I would have to earn it myself.

We were poor, but so were most people, so you didn't mind too much. My father, a lovable rogue, was a telegrapher on the railroad and always had a job somewhere. But most of his salary was spent on drinking and gambling and God-knows-what-all (according to my mother). When asked for current news of him or his present whereabouts, she most often answered tersely, "Daddy doesn't live with us." (That much was obvious, of course.) He rarely came to visit, either (probably because all hell was sure to break loose whenever he did). But my sister and I were sometimes allowed to visit him in the funny little backwater towns where he lived. Those were the best times. We adored our father.

My mother had been a beautiful woman when she was young, and my father had an eye for beautiful women. Once in a great while she talked about their courtship and marriage, when they were both employed in a large brokerage firm in San Francisco. She spoke wistfully of the lovely home they bought out near Golden Gate Park, and how well they lived on Daddy's $5,000-year salary (generous by 1920s standards). Then the stock market crashed and the Great Depression settled over the country like a black cloud.

My mother, 1920.

After so many years of worrying about how to make
ends meet, my mother was old at forty-five.

She had another, even more pressing worry. She was
German, and one of the first of her family to be born in
this country, I believe. After Pearl Harbor and the
clamor to put West Coast Japanese—regardless of
citizenship—in detention camps, euphemistically called
"relocation centers," there was a similar movement to

incarcerate Germans. Signs began appearing in and around Sacramento:

NOW THAT WE GOT THE JAPS OUT OF CALIFORNIA, LET'S GET THE GERMANS OUT, TOO!

My mother was afraid she might be sent away, and so was I. My father's impeccable English-American ancestry stretched back almost to the Mayflower, but one non-German parent might not be enough, so my sister and I were told what to say if anyone asked what nationality we were. And it went like this:

My mother's family had come from the Kingdom of Saxony (in Germany) and my father was Anglo, therefore we were *Anglo-Saxon*, not German.

For anyone who does not remember "the War," by which people of my generation always mean World War II, not Vietnam or any number of other wars, it must be nearly impossible to imagine what it was like in those days. In 1943 the only person I knew who had ever flown in an airplane was a young man my sister was dating. He was a pilot in the Air Force (or Air *Corps*, as it was called then). No one I knew owned a car. Cars were considered luxuries. Kids in the forties had no computer games or Barbie dolls or pricey footwear. There was no television. We played hopscotch on the sidewalk after school and kick-the-can in the street after dark. At parties we might play a daring game of spin the bottle. Or post office, where some-

The Alhambra Theater, exterior view.
Sacramento Public Library Collection.

one comes in and says, "I have a special delivery for
. . ." and a red-faced boy or girl would be led into the
next room to be kissed, amid the shrieks and whoops
of the rest of the party.

But if you had fifteen cents and a streetcar token on
a Saturday morning you could ride out to a palatial theater called the Alhambra and see cowboy movies and a
live stage performance by one of the local dance studios.

The Alhambra Theater, interior view.
Sacramento Public Library Collection.

I took tap and ballet at one of them, called "Miss Elizabeth's," and I was often part of the show on a Saturday morning. My mother, who sewed for Miss Elizabeth in exchange for my dance lessons, also made my costumes. We were not paid performers, of course, but being in the show had its advantages. For one thing, you got to stay and watch the movies for free.

I have said that my mother was a beautiful woman when she was young. My sister inherited our mother's dark beauty, but I was the image of my father with his sandy hair, green eyes, and freckles. Like him, I was lean and lanky. But my fifth-grade teacher, Mrs.

My sister, 1943.

1943 class picture, with me in the front row, second from left.

Coleman (a lady destined for sainthood, in my opinion), didn't hold with any such nonsense as heredity, and she decided that my skinny frame simply wanted nourishing. So, for that whole year she led me into the teachers' room each morning and bought me a pint of

E. E. SMITH

milk (extra rich) and a stack of graham crackers. Just to please her I would gladly have gained ten pounds, but I only grew taller.

It was already hot at eight o'clock that June morning when I skipped up the wide stone steps to the big old house for my interview with Mrs. Mumson. My hands were sweaty and my knees shook, but I tried to look cool and confident in a little cotton dress and white shoes. My mother, who also sewed for Mrs. Mumson, knew the lady needed a maid to replace the last one who had left to take a better-paying (and no doubt easier!) job as a riveter in the shipyard.

Beginning that day, and for nearly four months afterward, I would work harder than I had ever done before—or ever would do again. But we were living in extraordinary times. America was at war, there was a critical manpower shortage, and no one paid much attention to the child labor laws.

I was eleven years old.

CHAPTER TWO

MEETING MRS. MUMSON

At the top of the steps I suddenly froze. What caused my already shaky composure to fall apart completely was the realization that I had no idea what a maid actually *did.* I didn't know Mrs. Mumson, either. I thought of the times my mother had scolded my older sister for being selfish and "bone lazy," usually ending the tirade with this dire warning: "You'd better marry a rich man who can afford to hire a *maid!*" Was Mrs. Mumson like my sister? (It was not a comforting thought.) One thing I did know for sure. She was a tough customer of my mother's modest dressmaking business. Her trips to our house for fittings often left my mother cross and grumbling about ladies who were "cheap, penny-pinching, and demanding."

Should I run, or ring the bell? It was probably too late to run. Someone was sitting on the padded cushion of the bay window seat in the living room, not ten feet from where I stood on the porch. I was sure it was

Mrs. Mumson ("a plump, hard-to-fit figure"—my mother's words), and she may have seen me, too.

But Mrs. Mumson hadn't seen me. She was too busy arguing with someone, though as far as I could tell there was no one else in the room. I crept a little closer to the window in order to get a better view. From there I could also hear the conversation—at least her half of it, because that was all there was. I could see clearly now that she was alone and that she seemed to be addressing a portrait that hung above the sideboard in the dining room, beyond the parlor. I heard her saying, "Do I know there's a war on? My dear, if *I* don't, who *does*, I wonder?"—and then grumbling about shortages and having to keep track of everybody's ration books for food and all such like. She concluded with "it's the truth, Jack!" and began mopping her red face with her apron and fanning herself with a little pleated fan on a bamboo stick. Strands of damp gray hair had come loose from their pins and were hanging around her shoulders.

After another moment's hesitation to consider what it would be like, working for a lunatic in the habit of seeing ghosts (or at least talking to walls), I decided not to let a little thing like that stand in the way of buying a new bicycle.

I reached for the doorbell.

Wrenched out of her malaise at the sound of the bell, like an old fire horse or a prizefighter, Mrs.

Mumson rose abruptly from her seat and made for the front door. Then, as I watched, she did a curious thing. Returning to the window seat for a dish towel that had been lying on the cushion next to her, she began to wrap it around her arm, like a bandage. That done, she called out in a high, quavering voice, "Yes? Come in."

I opened the heavy front door. Inside, the wide hallway was hot and humid and smelled of a mixture of dust and mildew. A leaded glass window halfway up a staircase to one side provided the only light. Coming in from the bright sunshine to the gloom of the hall, I picked my way carefully along a threadbare carpet runner desperately in need of a good sweeping and came to a set of french doors. The glass panels looked as if they had not been washed since Herbert Hoover left office (*in other words, since before I was born*).

Not quite sure what to do next, I cautiously pushed open one of the french doors and tried to see what lay beyond. Three well-worn oak steps led down from the level of the hall to the parlor where the owner of the voice was standing.

"Mrs. Mumson . . . ?"

By now the lady was making an attempt, though largely unsuccessful, to recapture the loose strands of her hair as she took a few steps toward me. There hadn't been time to roll her sagging stockings back into the rubber garters that I guessed were just above her knees, under the dowdy housedress.

"Yes," she said in a soft, faintly southern accent. "I

do hope you'll excuse my somewhat untidy appearance, but I'm hardly able to do a *thing* with my arm this way, don't you know." Then, a closer look at the awkward child standing before her seemed first to surprise and then clearly disappoint her. "Oh!" she cried. "Are *you* Mrs. Smith's girl?"

"Yes, ma'am," I replied. I had been brought up to be polite to my elders (*too polite to ask what the heck was the matter with her arm, which had looked perfectly fine when I saw her through the window*).

Frowning, she said, "Your mother didn't tell me you were so *young!*"

"But I'm tall for my age," I protested.

"And what age is that?" she wanted to know.

"Well, I'm *going* on thirteen," I blurted out. "I'm strong, too! I can hit a baseball further than anyone in my class, even the boys! They call me Slugger Smith, and the outfielders back 'way up to the fence when it's my turn to bat."

Whether swayed by my enthusiasm or simply a lack of other candidates for the job, Mrs. Mumson appeared to relent. (She may also have been thinking of the stacks of dirty dishes in the kitchen rapidly becoming a health hazard.) In any case, she smiled and said, "Well, I can't very well call you 'Slugger,' now can I? What's your Christian name, dear?"

Having committed one crime (lying about my age) and seeing that I had not turned to stone, I decided to press my luck. "It's Eileen," I said boldly. Eileen was my middle name, so it was only half a lie. I hated my first name (and still do).

"Very well, Eileen," she said, motioning for me to follow her to the parlor, where she plunked her bulky frame down again on the window seat, "let's sit over here, shall we?" and then, hopefully, "there may be a little breeze."

But there wasn't. The air in the old house was as still as it was stale. Even the faded roses in the wallpaper seemed about to wilt, and the dusty gray curtains hung limp and motionless at the open windows.

Mrs. Mumson patted the cushion next to her, but I remained standing in the middle of the room, where I could get a better look at the portrait she had been conversing with earlier. I edged closer to it while she launched into a description of her "guests."

There were three "boys" and three "girls." She was chattering on about who they were and what they did ("Patsy's a stenographer and Iris is a welder, besides being the air raid warden for our block, don't you know . . ."), pausing only to ask me to fetch and carry for her—a cup of coffee from the badly tarnished silver urn on the sideboard in the dining room ("with *three* lumps of sugar, please, dear. I don't care if there *is* a war on!"), and a little throw pillow from the sofa. Clearly enjoying the service, she sighed contentedly, settled herself against the pillow, and sipped her coffee before picking up her train of thought. "Now, where was I? . . . Oh, yes. Our Margaret is 'a voice with a smile!' I guess you know what that is, don't you?"

I was only half listening to Mrs. Mumson, being more absorbed in a furtive investigation of the house, at least what I could see of it from where I stood.

The dining room held a large oak table with eight scuffed and mismatched chairs around it. There were also some overstuffed pieces that looked as if they belonged in the parlor but were crowded instead into the dining room. And there was the sideboard with the portrait over it. The man in it looked to be middle-aged and wore a bushy mustache and a uniform I couldn't identify at first. My mother had said that Mrs. Mumson was a widow. Could this be the late, lamented Mr. Mumson?

At the far end of the dining room was a swinging door which I felt sure would lead to an old-fashioned kitchen in this old-fashioned house. I noticed that the tall windows in the dining room had "blackout" curtains but there were none in the parlor. That would get you a citation from an air raid warden, and didn't she say there was one living right here in the house?

Suddenly realizing that Mrs. Mumson had asked me if I knew what a "voice with a smile" was, I reluctantly swung my attention back to her. "No, ma'am. I don't think I do."

"A telephone operator," she cried gleefully. "Haven't you seen those clever telephone company ads?" Then she checked herself. "Of course, poor Margaret hasn't been smiling much *lately!* Oh, you mustn't think I'm the kind of person who meddles in her guests' private lives! Gracious, no. But I confess I am worried about Margaret. And I nearly asked Doc to have a look at her, too, after I noticed she was positively green around the gills one morning at breakfast."

Did she mean there was a doctor living in the house? I hoped so. During the summer, especially, you were always worried about infantile paralysis. *Why, even Mr. Roosevelt had it, which meant no one was safe!*

"Well, we *call* him 'Doc,' even though he's still an intern," Mrs. Mumson explained. "In pediatrics."

That was all right. I knew what a pediatrician was, and even an intern would know polio if he saw it, wouldn't he?

"Then there's Howard," she continued. "Howard is a supervisor at the cannery. He and Teddy share the big bedroom at the front." She frowned. "We don't really know *what* Teddy does. We just hope it isn't anything illegal!" She paused, counting people on her fingers. "I did mention Iris, didn't I? She's the air raid warden. It was Iris's idea to move some of the parlor furniture into the dining room—the two big chairs, the lamp, the radio—to save having to buy blackout curtains for the parlor, don't you know."

Mrs. Mumson's character was becoming clearer to me, first from what my mother had said ("cheap, penny-pinching, demanding") and now saving money on blackout curtains for the parlor. I even imagined her asking my mother to make her a dress out of the ones in the dining room, once the war was over!

"Well, to begin with, Eileen, there's a lot to do here," declared Mrs. Mumson.

That was obvious. I made a mental list of things that needed doing in the downstairs alone (was it like this upstairs, too?). All the rugs that could be picked up and carried outside would get a good sweeping and airing. The oak furniture needed polishing. Those dusty curtains and the badly stained linen tablecloth would go into the washing machine (I hoped she had one!) before being starched and ironed. And if all the silverware was as black as that coffee urn . . . but here my thoughts were interrupted. Mrs. Mumson was laying out her own checklist of chores.

"There are five bedrooms—counting mine—to do up every morning after you've finished in the kitchen. Since Janet left me, the girls have been very good about doing their own rooms, but the boys . . . well, the boys don't seem to care very much. All except Howard, of course. Howard is very fussy about practically everything!" She frowned again. "I don't know how much longer I can keep Howard and Teddy in the same room. I feel certain they'll come to blows one of these days! The two girls seem to get along fine, but the boys—"

"My mother says girls are easier than boys."

"I dare say," agreed Mrs. Mumson. "Especially two such different ones! . . . Howard and Teddy, I mean.

You'll understand when you get to meet them." She had lost her train of thought again. "Now, where were we? . . . Oh, yes! Your mother said you had a bicycle, I believe?"

"Yes, ma'am. It's just my sister's old one. But it does have prewar tires."

It wasn't tires that Mrs. Mumson was interested in. She wanted to know if it had a sturdy basket. I said that it did. "Good. You can do the shopping. I'll give you a list of what to get. I've been having the markets deliver, but they charge an arm and a leg, and hardly ever get the whole order right! There's always something they forgot, or the eggs are broken, and I don't know what all!"

I was beginning to wonder if there would be time enough in the day to do everything this job required, when Mrs. Mumson seemed to read my mind.

"Oh, yes. There's a little room off the kitchen that Janet used. You can sleep there if it's all right with your mother. That way, you can get an earlier start of a morning!" Mrs. Mumson seemed to have thought of everything. "Well, that's settled, then. We give our guests breakfast and dinner six days a week, and put up lunch boxes for three of them, besides. They pay two dollars a week extra for that, of course."

In all this time she had never got around to mentioning how much I would be paid, and I was beginning to think she never would, for Mrs. Mumson was off on still another tack.

"I don't suppose you've done much cooking," she began hesitantly.

I was eager to set her straight on that point. "Oh, yes, I have! My sister can't boil water and my mother's too busy to cook, so I get most of the meals at home."

Mrs. Mumson brightened. "Really? What kinds of things can you cook?"

"Oh, golly, just about *anything*," I said with the confidence of one too young to know that a little knowledge is a dangerous thing. "I read Miss Kitchen in the paper. She tells you how to get the best meals with wartime shortages, how to use soybeans and low-point meats and stuff like that!"

Now the lady positively beamed! Low-point meats were the cheapest cuts, and soybeans cost practically nothing. But there was still the question of cooking for a large group. "You see, with my arm this way," she purred, "I'll be depending on you for everything!" (*No kidding*, I thought. But I was much too polite to say it.)

"And now about your salary." (*Finally!*) "Janet had been with me for years, so she got twenty-five dollars a week, but you'll get this new minimum wage of forty cents an hour." Then she added, "After a trial period, of course."

Well, Smarty Pants, how does a job in the tomato fields for sixty-five cents an hour, and only eight hours a day, look to you now?

Mrs. Mumson was thumbing the pages of the newspaper as she continued, "And you'll need a little uniform of some kind. I saw something in an ad just this morning for Hale Brothers . . . Yes, here it is. See? A pretty little frock with a white pinafore over it." She scowled at the price. "Four ninety-five? Tsk! Prices are just outrageous these days. Seems as if everybody is taking advantage of the war!" Folding the newspaper with the picture on the outside, she said, "Now, you take this home and show your mother. I'm sure she can make it for half that much."

I guessed that my mother would not welcome the challenge, but there was no alternative. Taking a whole five dollars out of the cookie jar to spend at Hale Brothers was unthinkable.

My employer was already looking ahead to the day she would be hiring someone to replace me. "And when do you have to go back to school, dear?"

"Not 'til the first of October. We get four months vacation this year. On account of the tomatoes." Mrs. Mumson did not immediately make the connection between vacations and tomatoes. "They need pickers," I explained. "I did that last summer. Pick tomatoes, I mean. It's pretty hard work but," I added slyly, "it *does* pay sixty-five cents an hour!" Of course she failed to take the hint. Had I really thought she might?

"Only four months," she mused. "And *then* what will we do, I wonder?" She gave a wistful little sigh before adding, "I suppose it's too much to hope that the war will be over in four months!" (In fact, it would last another three years.) "Well, the kitchen's this way, Eileen. You may as well start right in."

CHAPTER THREE

MEETING THE "BOYS"

Our progress toward the kitchen was interrupted by a sudden commotion outside the window overlooking the driveway. A car had pulled in, with brakes squealing and loud music playing on the radio.

"That must be Teddy," Mrs. Mumson observed matter-of-factly.

Just then another member of the household seemed to appear out of nowhere and swoop past us on his way to the window.

"Of course, it's Teddy!" he growled. "Who else would be making all that racket?"

I looked at the face, flushed with righteous indignation. His eyes flashed angrily behind wire-rimmed glasses. His dark hair had a plastered-down look. I had seen young men like him, in their white shirts and ties even on hot days, going around the neighborhood carrying Bibles and knocking on doors, asking for "just a few minutes of your time." Kids at school called them "Holy Rollers" and we would watch them putting up their tents on vacant lots for their revival meetings later on in the evening. Of course, our parents would never allow us to go to one.

Leaning out the window, he shouted, "HEY, SOBERJOWSKI! SHUT THAT THING OFF!" His stiff black pants were too short and I could see that he was wearing a mismatched pair of socks—one blue and one gray.

Mrs. Mumson scolded him mildly. "Howard! I don't know what the neighbors must be thinking, with all the—"

"WHAT'D YA SAY, HOWIE? CAN'T HEAR YA!" yelled another voice.

"I SAID SHUT THAT—" but Howard found himself shouting over complete silence from the driveway below. He turned back to Mrs. Mumson, wiping dust from the windowsill off his hands with a white handkerchief.

"Sorry, Mumsy. That guy gets my goat! Always making a big, loud spectacle of himself! Morals of an alley cat," he grumbled. "Out all night, coming home at this hour! . . . Not that I *mind* having the room all to myself most nights. Which reminds me. When am I going to get a private room? I don't like to mention it, but I *am* paying nine dollars a week, same as Iris and Doc. And they've got private rooms!"

Mrs. Mumson sighed. "I know, Howard. I was just telling Eileen . . . Oh, but I'm forgetting my manners!" and by way of introduction she said, "Eileen Smith—Howard Dillingham."

"Pleased to meet you," Howard mumbled, hardly noticing. "Listen, Mumsy, about that room—"

The slam of the big front door made us all jump. Footsteps were coming down the hall, and I turned expectantly toward the french doors. A second later they flew open and Teddy took the three steps down to the parlor with the grace of a dancer. He wasn't particularly tall (barely six feet, I imagined) and he wasn't so awfully handsome. *Not like a movie star, anyhow. Not like Errol Flynn or Clark Gable. Maybe Sonny Tufts, though!* His curly blond hair fell over his forehead and his deep-set eyes sparkled with mischief. Teddy *enjoys* getting Howard's goat, I thought. He does it on purpose! Then I noticed what he was wearing—an outrageous getup of loud black-and-white checkered pants and a black shiny vest over a polo shirt. I was mesmerized.

"Hi ya, Mumsy!" Teddy said with a wink. Then, turning to Howard he said without noticeable malice, "Hey, Howie! What time's the meetin' tonight?"

Howard sniffed, "Poking fun at a person's religion is not funny, Soberjowski!" and Teddy shot back with, "Yeah? Well, neither are your Polack jokes!"

Mrs. Mumson said fretfully, "I do wish you two would try to get along!"

Doing my best to make myself invisible during all of this, I moved in behind Mrs. Mumson and waited for my chance to slip through the swinging door to the kitchen.

Teddy yawned and said, "Hope I'm not too late for breakfast, Mumsy. I've had a hard night!"

Howard snorted, "I can imagine!" Then, pointing out the window he said, "Now, where'd you get *that* car? In an all-night poker game down at the pool hall, right?"

"Wrong," Teddy said casually. "Make it Bingo. In the church basement."

My father always said you had to know when to hold, and know when to fold. You could tell Howard didn't know when to fold.

"That's the fourth car you've had in six months! And with a 'C' card in the window! How do you rate a 'C' card? Just what kind of business are you in, anyways?"

"Used cars," said Teddy, pretending to study his nails.

With a sneer Howard said, "Is that why you always dress like *Moon Mullins?*"

Teddy quickly shot back with, "Hey, look who's talking! One of the *Katzenjammer Kids!*"

I couldn't help it. I was suddenly seized with a bad case of the giggles.

"Whoa!" said Teddy, looking around. "Who're you hiding back there, Mumsy?"

Mrs. Mumson seemed to have forgotten all about me. Looking confused, she said, "What?" Then remembering, she pushed me gently out in front of her and said, "Oh! This is Eileen Smith, Teddy. She's going to be my helper this summer."

For the first time, Teddy shone his radiant smile my

way. I suddenly felt all hands and feet. "I knew a girl named Eileen once," he said disarmingly. "But she wasn't near as pretty as you!"

"Oh, brother," groaned Howard, rolling his eyes.

My face was burning. Not usually at a loss for words, I tried desperately to think of something to say, but my brain refused to cooperate. Edging closer to the window, I suddenly gasped, "*Gol-leee!* A red convertible! And about a block long! Is it brand new?"

The red convertible.
Courtesy of the Automobile Quarterly Research and Photo Archives.

Teddy joined me at the window. "No, not quite, Smitty. It's a '41. Maybe the last of those big fat beauties to roll off the assembly line. Since then they've gone over to making tanks for Uncle Sam." I was still gaping at the car and Teddy saw a chance to make a little girl happy. "Say! How 'bout you and me going for a spin later on? After dinner, maybe."

"That's our Teddy," sneered Howard. "A wolf in wolf's clothing!"

"Aw, dry up, Bird Brain," growled Teddy.

"That's enough, you two!" scolded Mrs. Mumson. "Eileen can do whatever she likes on her own time, but right now she has work to do in the kitchen."

"Boy, howdy!" exclaimed Teddy, who must have seen the kitchen recently. "By the way, Mumsy, what's with the broken wing act?"

Mrs. Mumson looked puzzled. "The what?" Then, glancing down at the dish towel still wrapped around her arm, she colored slightly before she said, "Oh, this? Well, I'm sure it's only a *sprain*, Teddy."

Silently, in his crepe-soled shoes, a young man in a white lab coat with a stethoscope stuffed in the pocket had approached Mrs. Mumson from behind. I swear she jumped a foot when he spoke to her.

"Want me to have a look at it, Mumsy?" asked the young man. Except for the white coat and stethoscope you wouldn't have taken him for a doctor. He had red hair and freckles on his nose, but his bright blue eyes were alert and kind. Sort of sad, too, I thought.

Mrs. Mumson recovered enough to say, "Oh! Good morning, Doc. Mercy! You startled me . . . Going to the hospital? Better have some breakfast first."

Looking at his watch, Doc said, "Right. Thanks.

Just anything, as long as it's quick." Then he added, "Oh, and don't expect me for dinner tonight. I'll get a bite at the hospital."

Mrs. Mumson was concerned. "What is it, Doc? Some sort of emergency?"

His answer temporarily drove all thoughts of the beautiful red convertible out of my head. "Infantile paralysis," he said gravely. "And starting to look like an epidemic. We've had four new cases just since the first of June."

"I'll get you something right away," Mrs. Mumson said, hurrying out through the swinging door. "Eileen, you can pour Doc a cup of coffee."

Doc was holding a small black bag, which he put down next to a chair at the table. "That's all right, Eileen," he said, smiling and reaching for the coffee urn on the sideboard. When he had poured himself a cup, he sat down next to his bag.

I thought he looked very tired.

"Will they close the pool again this summer?" I asked. The municipal pool was a prime suspect as a source of exposure to polio among children.

"I'm afraid so. Just until they feel there's no more danger." *But that would be all summer! Well, never mind. I wouldn't have time to go swimming anyway, with my new twenty-four-hour-a-day job!* Doc explained that it was better to be safe than sorry. "You know about polio, don't you?"

"Sure," I said. *What kid my age didn't?*

"There are some things you can do to protect your-self. It's best that you know what they are."

"You mean, like getting enough rest and changing my shoes if they get wet?" *I had read that someplace.*

"That's right. It's especially important not to get too tired. And if you get a headache or feel like you have a fever, you want to let someone know right away. Will you do that?"

"Yes, sir," I said respectfully. My mother was a Christian Scientist, and I had never been to a doctor, so far as I knew. I wondered if they were all as nice as this young intern with the kind, sad eyes.

"Well, when you can't go swimming," Teddy said, lounging with his elbows on the table, "what do you do for fun, Smitty?" Then with a wink he added, "Besides working in a boardinghouse, I mean."

I thought for a moment. "Well, for one thing, I like to dance. I take lessons from a dance studio in my neighborhood."

"Yeah? What kind?"

"Oh, tap. Ballet. Stuff like that."

"No kidding?"

"I tap dance sometimes at the Alhambra," I said proudly. "On Saturday mornings."

"In some kind of talent show, you mean?"

"No, it's called 'live entertainment' between the cartoons and the cowboy movies."

"Say, I'd like to see that! I've always had a soft spot for tap dancers."

Howard snorted, "Your soft spot is your *head*, Soberjowski!" but Teddy ignored him.

Mrs. Mumson returned from the kitchen, carrying a tray. "Here you are, Doc. I hope Post Toasties and cream will be all right. It was the quickest thing I could think of."

The dish towel was slipping off her arm. I caught it before it hit the floor.

CHAPTER FOUR

MEETING THE "GIRLS"

The relative calm that had descended over the dining room in the past few minutes was soon shattered by the noisy arrival of another strange bird in Mrs. Mumson's flock.

The big front door banged shut, followed by heavy footsteps in the hall. I looked up, expecting to see a man. Instead it was a woman, dressed like men you saw in the newsreels. The legs of her baggy khaki jumpsuit were tucked into a pair of thick boots. She pulled off a white helmet with "CD" in black letters on the front, exposing her short straight hair. Like the helmet, a canvas bag hanging on her shoulder also displayed the Civil Defense emblem. Skipping the first two steps down into the parlor, she crash-landed on the third. Iris the air raid warden was home.

"Oh, Iris, dear," Mrs. Mumson sang out, as the newcomer strode noisily into the dining room, "you must be exhausted, watching out for enemy planes all night!

I'm sure I couldn't stay awake! Let me get you a cup of coffee. Was there any excitement last night?"

"Yeah, Iris. Spot any Messerschmitts over the community clubhouse?" Teddy deadpanned.

Iris dropped the heavy canvas bag on the floor next to a chair and regarded Teddy with cold contempt. "Too bad *you* don't do something for the war effort, Soberjowski. Like volunteering for a suicide mission!" Then, pointing to the cup Mrs. Mumson had poured for her, she said, "Hold on a minute, Mums! Why are we still drinking coffee? Mrs. Roosevelt isn't serving anything but tea for the duration. If it's good enough for the *White House*—"

Teddy cut her off with, "Aw, keep your shorts on, Iris. Even Mrs. Roosevelt still serves coffee for breakfast. The *rest* of the day she serves tea. Read the papers."

Iris ignored him. "By the way, Mums, they're going to start testing the air raid sirens this month. Twenty-second blasts at seven o'clock in the evening. After the system gets up and running, a two-minute siren will mean a blackout, a one-minute will signal the all-clear. Got that?"

Mrs. Mumson looked blank. "Oh, dear," she said, gnawing her lip.

Iris said impatiently, "Now, pay attention, Mums! This is important," and she explained it all again, ending with, "Can't have my own people doing the wrong thing! When that two-minute siren goes off, *my* job is to go out and see that the rest of the block is blacked out," and with a sweeping gesture toward the dining room windows, "*your* job is to pull those curtains down and keep 'em down until you hear the one-minute all-clear. Okay," she continued, hauling her leg over a chair at the table, "we need to lay in a supply of candles and flashlights, too." Then, noticing me for the first time, she said, "Who's that?"

Mrs. Mumson started to tell her, but Iris was already forging ahead, like a general briefing the troops before battle, "And about the gas masks. You can each buy your own or I'll buy enough for all of us, and you can pay me later." That done, she turned again to Mrs. Mumson. "Oh, and Mums! Do you have plenty of Clorox? You'd better get several large bottles. We know that Clorox can neutralize liquid mustard gas!"

Glancing again at his watch, Doc excused himself from the table, picked up his black bag, and turned to go. But he must have seen the look of wide-eyed terror on my face, because he smiled reassuringly and said, "Don't let Iris scare you, honey."

Teddy chimed in with, "Yeah, Iris. Lay off the Clorox and the mustard gas 'til I'm done with my Post Toasties, will ya?"

In vivid contrast to Iris's boots, a pair of high-heeled sandals now came clicking down the steps into the parlor, attached to the legs of a beautiful blonde. She was all curves and girlishness in a pair of white shorts and a little blue sweater that just reached to her waist. I thought of Lana Turner or maybe even Betty Grable with those legs.

What happened next was right out of Vaudeville. With his eyes on the pin-up girl, instead of where he was going, Doc slammed into the sideboard. The dishes inside rattled for several seconds, while his face turned the color of his hair.

The girl smiled apologetically and said, "Oh, golly! I'm sorry, Doc. Did I do that?"

Thoroughly flustered, Doc stammered, "No, no! My fault! Sorry! Well . . . goodbye," and bolted out through the french doors, but not before tripping over the third step.

Teddy was shaking his head. "Do us all a favor, Patsy. Marry that poor guy. And do it before he breaks everything in the house!"

Patsy's tone was cool but not unfriendly, "Are you writing a lonely hearts column now, Teddy?"

"Listen, it doesn't take a sob sister to see that old Doc has got it *bad*—and that ain't *good!*"

Patsy advanced toward the table as Teddy got up, stretching and saying he thought he'd go upstairs and get a little shut-eye. The two passed each other in the middle of the dining room. Teddy put his hands on Patsy's shoulders and said, close to her ear, "Watch out, Glamour Puss. Iris will have that pretty face in a gas mask before you can say, 'A slip of the lip can sink a ship!'" As he went out, he called back over his shoulder, "Hey, Smitty! We'll go for that spin after dinner!"

Looking around, Patsy said, "Smitty? Who's Smitty?"

Mrs. Mumson explained, and Patsy said with a grin, "Gonna be part of our little soap opera, huh?" Then, melodramatically, "The story that asks the question: Can a little girl from . . . Where do you live, Smitty?"

"Twenty-fifth and P," I giggled.

". . . from Twenty-fifth and P, find happiness in Ma Mumson's boardinghouse?"

Using the word "boardinghouse" in Mrs. Mumson's presence was tantamount to swearing. "Patsy!" she said sharply.

"Oh, before I forget, Mumsy, maybe you should check on Margaret. She's looking green around the gills again," and sitting down at the table she said, "Any Post Toasties left? Is that real cream? . . . Pardon my boardinghouse reach!"

Twice in one morning was too much for Mrs. Mumson. "Patsy," she said irritably, "you know I don't like that word. Kindly do not use it to describe my *guest* house."

"Sorry, Mumsy."

"You say Margaret isn't looking well again this morning?"

"But def!" replied Patsy the hep cat.

Mrs. Mumson frowned. "Maybe I *should* ask Doc to take a look at her when he gets—"

But Iris cut her off with, "Pshaw, Mums!" Her mouth was full of cereal at the time, resulting in a small shower of flakes on the tablecloth. "Every time a body gets a toothache around here is no cause for you to get yourself all worked up."

Howard, who had been paying close attention for the last couple of minutes, abruptly got up from the table. "I'll see you later," he said to no one in particular. As he jogged up the steps to the front hall he turned and said, "Don't forget what we talked about, Mumsy."

"What's with him?" asked Patsy, when Howard had disappeared through the french doors.

Mrs. Mumson explained that Howard had been pressing his demand for a private room. "But he knows I don't have one to give him," she sighed.

"Here's an idea, Mums." Iris was wiping cream off her chin. "Why not let Howard have my room? I could bunk in with you. You've got two beds. And I could use the extra buck and a half."

You could tell that Mrs. Mumson was torn between the prospect of peace between Howard and Teddy, on the one hand, and the loss of privacy (not to mention the dollar and a half a week!), on the other. But at last she seemed reconciled. "All right, Iris, I'll tell Howard he can have your room." Turning to me, she said, "Eileen, you can take the tray and gather up the dirty dishes. You'll find a few more in the kitchen from last night, too."

That turned out to be the understatement of the year.

❖ ❖ ❖

The swinging door to the kitchen did not close all the way on its rusty hinges, stopping short by about two inches. Even as I tackled the mess in the kitchen I could hear the dining room conversation through the gap.

"Say, Patsy," Iris was saying, "we've got a new course in Aircraft Recognition starting next week. Want to become a spotter?"

"No can do, Iris. I'm taking a night course."

This was a bit of news that Mrs. Mumson had some-how missed. "Really, Patsy? What kind of a course?"

Patsy said it was a course in Japanese, and Iris shouted, "*Japanese!* What the hell *for?*"

That brought a quick "tsk, tsk!" from Mrs. Mumson. Swearing was against the house rules.

Patsy explained that she had read in the paper where they were looking for women with six months or more of training in the Japanese language. After tak-ing the course and a qualifying exam for the Navy's interpreter program, she could get a commission in the WAVES.

Mrs. Mumson seemed to take it personally. "Does that mean you'll be leaving us?" she whined. "And why do they want *white* people, anyway? Why don't they just use—"

Iris jumped in with, "I know what you're going to say, Mums," without waiting for her to say it. "Why not use *Japs* as interpreters? Because you can't trust 'em, *that's* why!"

Patsy said they *did* use Japanese interpreters, but Iris stubbornly refused to believe it.

Mrs. Mumson said it was too bad "little Yukie" wasn't here to help Patsy learn the language, adding that the garden had never looked the same since he had been sent away to "that camp." Iris argued that they could all sleep better at night, knowing that Yukie and his "slanty-eyed little friends" were safely behind bars. But Mrs. Mumson seemed troubled. "Now, Iris, I can't believe that Yukie Matsumoto would ever do this country any harm. It was his country, too! He was an American citizen, just like the rest of us."

Iris said a Jap was a Jap, and she bet some of them got to *be* citizens just so they could serve the emperor. Patsy said Iris didn't know what she was talking about. Japanese couldn't *become* citizens—they'd have to be born here.

"So? How do you know some of 'em weren't born here just so they could grow up to be spies?"

"Oh, that's rich, Iris! Mr. Roosevelt needs *you* for his Brain Trust!"

Mrs. Mumson declared that she just knew little Yukie would never be disloyal, and Iris said, "No? Did he ever say who he thought would win the war?" and before Mrs. Mumson could answer, "There's this story about a Jap gardener leaving for the camp, see? The lady he works for says to him, 'After the war you can have your old job back,' and the Jap says to her, 'No, missy! After war I no work for *you!* You work for *me!'"*

Mrs. Mumson said it still didn't seem fair, don't you know, and Iris shouted, *"Fair?* Flora Mumson! Don't you know there's a *war* on?"

"But the way they made the whole family pick up and leave their little flower shop. And their house. And their land, too! . . . I just don't think it was fair!"

I could hear Iris pounding the table. "We had to get those people out of California. They were forming their own fifth column, sure as shootin'!"

By this time I had enough clean dishes to carry a tray of them into the dining room. Pushing open the swinging door, I asked innocently, "What's a fifth column?"

"Spies!" declared Iris hotly. "A network of enemy aliens! Ready to turn on this country at a given signal from the Axis!"

Patsy rolled her eyes and pursed her bright red lips.

I asked what had happened to the boy named Yukie, and Mrs. Mumson explained that they just called him that because he played the ukulele. They never knew his real name. "Anyway, he's in a detention camp now."

Next to polio, the thing I feared most in my young life was being sent away when they rounded up the Germans. I suddenly blurted out, "My mother says *we* might be sent to a concentration camp!"

"Why, mercy, child!" cooed Mrs. Mumson, "you're not Japanese!"

I told how my mother was German and afraid of being incarcerated, along with the Japanese. We were citizens, of course, but a lot of them were, too.

"I don't think you have to worry, Smitty," said Patsy, glaring at Iris. "We haven't lost our heads *completely!*"

"Just the same, Patsy, evacuation was the only way to deal with the 'yellow peril.' Don't you read Walter Lippman?"

Patsy said, yes, and the *real* "yellow peril" was the color of his journalism.

Iris shot back with, "Well, don't forget the attack on Goleta!"

"Come on, Iris! A round of shells lobbed into a tomato field! From a Japanese sub? In the Santa Barbara Channel?" Iris started to protest, but Patsy was too quick for her. "Look, let's say that it *was* a Japanese sub that fired those shells. Where were all your 'fifth columnists' *then?* Why didn't they rise up and join the attack?" With Iris silenced for the moment, she turned to me. "It would be a lot harder to evacuate the Germans than it was the Japanese. For one thing, it's not easy to *tell* a German."

"My father says it's not easy to tell a German *any-thing!*"

Patsy laughed and said, "No, honey. What I meant was, it's not easy to tell a German from anybody *else.*"

Iris scraped her chair away from the table and got up to leave. "Okay, Patsy, go ahead and laugh," she growled, "but I hope the WAVES knock some sense into your head!" Pointing a finger at Mrs. Mumson, she said, "Don't forget to write Clorox down on your grocery list, Mums. And get the biggest bottles they have!"

Iris stomped out, and Patsy turned to Mrs. Mumson, "Big bottles of Clorox? What for?"

"Oh, Iris says it neutralizes mustard gas, or something."

"Terrif!" snarled Patsy. "You'd think this was Iris Dozier's private war. What do you want to bet she's a member of the Home Front Commandos?"

"The Home Front what?"

"Commandos. Where's this morning's paper? . . . Here. Listen to this. 'Wanted. Men and women for soliciting new members for the Home Front Commandos, an organization whose objective is to deport the Japs after the war.'"

"Mercy!" gasped Mrs. Mumson.

"'Workers will be compensated. Write today for appointment. Give age, references, occupation, etc.— Help organize a chapter in your community!'"

Now I was really worried! "Will they deport the Germans, too?"

Mrs. Mumson said no, of course not, and shooed me back into the kitchen. "Little pitchers have big ears," she said, and started talking more quietly after that. (But I could still hear through the gap in the swinging door.) "I'd like a word with you on another matter, Patsy. A delicate one, I'm afraid."

"Sure, Mumsy. Shoot!"

"It's about Margaret. I've been thinking. Do you suppose she could be in 'a family way?'"

"In a what?"

"You know what I mean. As her roommate, don't you know, I thought she might have confided something of a personal nature to you."

Patsy said she didn't know Margaret *had* a personal nature, and Mrs. Mumson said she just wondered whether Margaret had "gotten herself into trouble."

That got a rise out of Patsy. She said that no girl ever gets *herself* into trouble. "It's usually a team effort."

But Mrs. Mumson would not be put off. "You know what I mean," she said again.

"But Margaret's so shy and—let's face it, she's not heavy on *glam*—the kind of girl that boys never even notice, much less get *pee-gee!*"

Mrs. Mumson said she hoped she was wrong, but if not, well, she just couldn't have "that sort of thing" going on under her own roof! Why, just imagine what Mr. Mumson would say! Not to mention the neighbors.

"You mean you think Margaret and one of the boys here . . . but who?"

Mrs. Mumson reminded her that there was *one* boy here who didn't care two pins about rules, and didn't care who knew it, either!

"You mean Teddy? Margaret and Teddy? Don't be ridic! . . . Okay, so Teddy's a wolf, but Margaret's just not his type! She's, y'know, kind of mousy."

A streetcar in a Sacramento residential neighborhood.
Courtesy the California State Railroad Museum.

Mrs. Mumson sighed and said she was afraid that kind of girl was the most vulnerable.

"Uh-oh," said Patsy. "Sounds like she's coming down. And I'm late already. They've got real nylon stockings at Weinstock's today. The line will be all around the block by the time I get there. What's the next streetcar, Mumsy?"

Mrs. Mumson said it was the 8:55 out of the car barn, passing the house at 9:30 sharp. Patsy laughed and called her a "walking timetable," but Mrs. Mumson said, "Well, this was Mr. Mumson's route, don't you know." Hearing that, I suddenly remembered where I had seen a uniform like the one in the portrait in the dining room. The streetcar operators wore them.

I pushed open the swinging door an inch or two further so I could get a look at Margaret when she came down. In a moment, a girl wearing a drab flannel bathrobe tied loosely around the waist with a braided cord shuffled into the dining room in a pair of flat, fuzzy slippers. Her face was pale (*I was straining to see if it was "green around the gills," wherever that was*). She wore her dull brown hair wound loosely into a bun at the back of her neck, like Miss Rooney, the librarian at my school.

Patsy greeted her warmly, "Oh, hi, Margaret! I was just saying I thought I'd run downtown this morning and try to get some real stockings." If Margaret heard her, she showed no sign of it, so Patsy went on, "Those baggy rayons are enough to make a girl start painting her legs! Only, I tried a bottle of that leg makeup and it rubbed off all over my skirt! Wanna come along?"

The idea that the mousy girl in the bathrobe would give a hoot about what she wore on her legs seemed pretty silly to me! I could barely hear her when she said, "No thanks. You go ahead."

"Well, okay," Patsy said. Then she turned and danced up the steps to the front hall with a cheery, "Plant you now, dig you later!"

Margaret drifted into a chair at the table and began pouring cereal into a bowl. Mrs. Mumson did her best to make conversation. "I wish Patsy would meet some nice boy and settle down, don't you, Margaret?" There was no answer, but Mrs. Mumson persisted. "Such a sweet girl, even if she *is* a little wild!"

Margaret's answer to that took Mrs. Mumson by surprise. "And *I'm* going to be wild if anyone else tells me how sweet Patsy is!" she snapped.

"Oh, my!" said Mrs. Mumson, as if talking to a child. "Did we get up on the wrong side of our bed this morning?"

Margaret said she was sorry, but Mrs. Mumson wasn't satisfied. "Now, don't tell me you and Patsy have been quarreling! Haven't I got enough trouble with Teddy and Howard?"

Margaret said they hadn't been quarreling. Only it wasn't fair that girls like Patsy—the pin-up girls—had everything. "Well, no one ever said *women* were created equal, did they?" Then, pushing the cereal bowl away, she said she guessed she wasn't hungry.

Mrs. Mumson told her she really ought to have a proper breakfast and to sit right there while she fixed her something hot. I suddenly realized she was about to push open the swinging door—*and me with my nose right up against it!* I just managed to jump out of the way, and grab a tray of clean dishes at the same time. As Mrs. Mumson brushed by me, I said, "I was just taking these in."

Margaret looked startled to see a stranger coming out of the kitchen. "Oh!" she said, shyly closing the robe tightly around her neck. "I didn't know there was anyone else in the house."

"Heck, I'm not anyone," I assured her. "I work here. Just since this morning."

"Oh, I see. What's your name?"

"Eileen Smith. But Teddy calls me 'Smitty!'" I knew I was beginning to blush again, thinking about Teddy Soberjowski, the red convertible, and going for a spin after dinner. I hoped she hadn't noticed.

"Teddy likes to make up names for people. He calls me 'Magpie,' but my name is really Margaret." There were dark circles under her mousy brown eyes and she seemed almost too tired to talk, so I turned away and began stacking dishes on the sideboard. All the time I was thinking about what Mrs. Mumson had said: "Of course, poor Margaret hasn't been smiling much *lately!*"

When the tray was empty, I turned back to her and said, "I guess you must be the 'voice with a smile!'" *Trust me to say the wrong thing!*

Margaret scowled and said, "Oh, you've seen those idiotic telephone ads."

I tried another approach. "If I pick up the phone, are you the one that says, 'Number please?'" (*I said it like "pleee-uzz," pinching my nose like a clothespin. And she smiled!*)

"No. I'm an overseas operator. We don't say that."

"You mean you get to talk to Europe and places like that?"

She said she did. I wanted to know if she had to talk to people in a foreign language. "Well, just things like, 'I'll connect you with your party now.' Mostly in French, Spanish, or German."

I wanted to tell Margaret that I could speak a little German, too (my grandmother had taught me a few phrases, behind my mother's back) but what if she took me for a German spy or a—what was it?—a fifth columnist!

Before I had time to think about it, Mrs. Mumson returned from the kitchen.

"There now, I've got an egg boiling for you, Margaret. I see you've met Eileen." Then she told me to take the egg out of the water in two minutes "and mind you don't let the toast burn!"

Back in the kitchen I heard most of what was said in the dining room while I timed the egg and kept a close watch on the toast.

Mrs. Mumson was offering Margaret a cup of coffee, saying, "If Iris has *her* way, we won't be drinking it much longer, so we'd better enjoy it while we can!" Then she spied the mailman coming up the walk and got him to hand the mail to her through the window so she wouldn't have to go out to the box. A moment later she exclaimed, "Here's a card from my daughter. The doctor says the baby could come any time now! Oh, dear! If only Janet had stayed on a few more weeks! Can you see little Eileen coping with everything here for a month or so while I'm away? And where would I get anyone else?" She ended with her favorite rant about not being able to get domestic help nowadays because they were all in the shipyards.

The egg was done and the toast buttered. I added my own secret ingredient, which I had found in the cupboard, and proudly carried the tray into the dining room.

Margaret took one look and said, "Oh! What *is* that?"

I could see what she meant. It did look a little weird. "The egg is that funny brown color because I stirred some peanut butter into it. Miss Kitchen—she's in the paper—says that peanut butter is a good source of protein in these days of meat shortages!"

Margaret suddenly got up and bolted out of the dining room with her hand over her mouth.

Mrs. Mumson noticed my look of dismay and said, "Never mind, dear. Margaret just didn't feel like testing any wartime recipes this morning!" And she must have known what I was thinking, too—that it was a shame to waste a perfectly good breakfast (especially when I hadn't had any)—because she said, "Would you like to have it?" and then added a little disdainfully, "Children can eat . . . almost anything."

I nodded eagerly and pushed the tray to an empty place at the end of the table. Already attacking the toast and jam as I sat down, I nearly choked as Mrs. Mumson shrieked, "Oh, don't sit *there!*"

I jumped up again, thinking I had sat on some priceless antique (as unlikely as it seemed). Mrs. Mumson apologized for speaking so sharply and then explained, as I gingerly settled into another place at the table, that I had sat in Mr. Mumson's chair, which was always kept vacant for *him*. She pointed out that his picture hung directly above that particular chair and she could imagine him sitting there, just as if he were still with her. *I thought that was kind of nice. At the same time it gave me the creeps.*

"My, but he was handsome," she went on, gazing fondly at the portrait. Scraping up the last of the peanut-buttery egg, I looked up and tried to imagine Mr. Mumson as a young, handsome man. "But then, my father always *said* my head would be turned by a man in a uniform!"

To be polite, although I was pretty sure I knew already, I asked what kind of a uniform it was. Mrs. Mumson clapped her plump white hands together and said, with a girlish giggle, "Why, the uniform of a municipal railway engineer!"

Then I heard the story of how she came to leave her family in the idyllic setting somewhere on the east coast and wind up here.

"Mr. Mumson drove a streetcar, you see. As a matter of fact, I *met* him on a streetcar!" (I wondered if he was driving it at the time, but thought I'd better not ask.) "He was attending a Motorman's Convention in my home town," she went on to explain. She had been engaged to a Charleston man at the time—one Chester A. Gump—but Mr. Mumson had just swept her off her

The California state capitol and grounds.
Sacramento Public Library Collection.

feet, and she soon forgot all about poor Chester. When he proposed, Mr. Mumson said he would take her to live "in the shadow of the Capitol" and she was thrilled. Her face fell slightly as she added, "Of course, he meant the *state* capitol here in Sacramento, and I had in mind the *U.S.* Capitol in Washington, D.C!" Gazing at the portrait again she sighed, "But we had thirty wonderful years together, didn't we, Jack?"

Coming out of her reverie and returning to the present once more, she pointed to my empty plate and said,

"Well now, dear, if you've finished that *concoction* of yours, I expect there are still things to do in the kitchen."

There were, of course. I picked up my tray and headed for the swinging door, as she sang out cheerfully, "Idle hands are the devil's playground, don't you know!"

Back at the sink, I knew Mrs. Mumson had switched on the radio in the dining room. First there was a loud buzz, then crinkly static, and finally the voice of a radio announcer: "Is the sweetheart you married the husband you expected him to be? Has the war created new problems for you in your marriage? To answer these and other questions brought in by your friends and neighbors, Arrid Underarm Deodorant presents John J. Anthony, founder of the famed Marriage Relations Institute, in a brand-new program of daily sessions of kindly and helpful advice!"

I heard Mrs. Mumson sigh contentedly and settle herself in the creaky leather armchair next to the old radio.

"But first a word from our sponsor . . ."

CHAPTER FIVE

WAVING THE FLAG

I had worked for Mrs. Mumson for about a month by the Fourth of July holiday. Not that it was a holiday for me. I had no holidays. One day a week (usually a Saturday) was all I could call my own. I had danced with my tap class on the stage of the Alhambra Theater only once since school let out. My teacher at Miss Elizabeth's was complaining. So was my mother. She said the room my sister and I shared looked like a pigsty now that I was sleeping at the boardinghouse. My sister said it wasn't *her* fault that I was not there to pick up after her!

But I had my own priorities. I spent every waking hour putting Mrs. Mumson's house in order. And now the linen tablecloth and the curtains at the tall windows were snowy white again, the silverware and the coffee urn shone in the sun streaming through sparkling clean windows, the furniture was polished, the floors and rugs swept. Meals were served on time, even if they were not to everyone's taste.

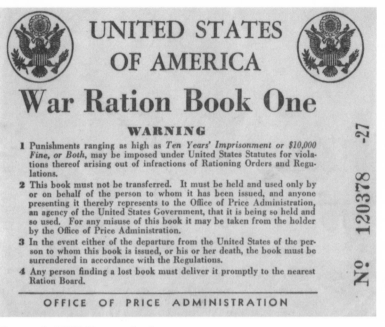

Cover of a WW II ration book.

My devotion to Miss Kitchen, and the wartime recipes in her column, were under fire from all sides. Everyone was sympathetic—up to a point—with the strain that rationing put on even the most experienced cooks during the war. Eight ration books, including my own, were kept in a drawer in the sideboard. They contained a bewildering array of red, green, and blue stamps (plus gray ones marked "spares," to add to the confusion). Without these you couldn't buy meat, butter, canned goods, coffee, or sugar. Not unless you wanted to trade on the black market, which was illegal, not to mention unpatriotic. To keep track of everyone's ration books and, ideally, to avoid running out of

A "Home Front Pledge" from the *Sacramento Bee*.

stamps before the end of the month, was no easy task. Still, some of my meals *a la* Miss Kitchen met with resistance. Meatless Meat Loaf, for example (made with soybeans).

I usually went to bed in the little room off the kitchen at midnight, then rose before the sun was up, the coolest part of the day. I had little time for anything except the job of running the house. Obviously I could have done less, but I was proud of how clean and orderly things were now. Teddy called me a real live Snow White, keeping house for the Seven Dwarfs (six boarders and Mrs. Mumson). If I was working too hard and my health was suffering, well, whose fault was that? *It was Daddy's!* My mother said I had inherited a "fastidious gene" from him.

My father, George "Paddy" Smith.

George "Paddy" Smith was known as a dapper gentleman. His shoes were always polished to a mirror finish. He wore a well-brushed fedora and a gold watch on a chain across his vest. As a railroad telegrapher he had free housing, often in the train station itself. Such quarters were always Spartan and some, especially in the more remote towns where he worked, lacked such basic amenities as indoor plumbing—hardly the habitat of a dapper gentleman! But under my father's care, the place would be spotless.

By this time there were other, more subtle changes taking place in the boardinghouse. For one thing, I was no longer self-conscious or shy around Teddy. We had become pals, though I couldn't have said why, exactly. Maybe he thought of me as a kid sister. Maybe he didn't like to see a little girl work so hard and never have any fun. *I hoped and prayed it was 'cause he liked me!* Whatever the reason, he took me on jaunts around town in his car (he seemed to have a new one every week). We laughed and sang along with the music on his car radio. I began to think of Teddy as my knight in shining armor, rescuing me from the drab prison walls of the boardinghouse. But the others, especially Howard and Iris, still considered him a pain in the neck.

That Fourth of July started out much like any other. The day was a scorcher, even for Sacramento. The heat and humidity made the air in the dining room almost too heavy to breathe. Mrs. Mumson's six "guests," seated around the table waiting for dinner to be served, were visibly wilting, along with my special red, white, and blue centerpiece. Everyone had come downstairs dressed in his or her holiday best. All except Iris, that is. She was wearing her usual olive drab, with the Civil Defense bag and helmet slung over her chair.

Most days I had the kitchen all to myself, but the occasion of a special holiday dinner had prompted the lady of the house to make a rare appearance that afternoon. *And if they thought it was hot in the dining room, they should have been out there in the kitchen with us!*

Howard complained that Mrs. Mumson really ought to buy a fan for the dining room. He was burning up! Teddy had some advice for him. "Try ditching the undershirt, Howie. Nobody wears an undershirt anymore. Didn't you see *It Happened One Night?* I couldn't hear what Howard said, but Teddy went on to say, "Oh, I forgot. You don't go to movies, do ya? Too bad. You might learn something. Anyway, that's where Clark Gable takes off his shirt, see, and he's not wearing an undershirt. Overnight, guys stopped wearing undershirts."

Howard said he didn't know where Teddy got off advising *anybody* about what to wear.

Tempers continued to rise faster than the temperature. Teddy dropped the subject of undershirts, but went on needling Howard. (It was one of his favorite pastimes.) "You've been busier than a pig in a corncrib today, Howie. All moved into Iris's room?"

Howard's reply was a sullen, "Not quite, but I'm sleeping there tonight."

I could imagine the smirk on Teddy's face when he said, "Better not get too cozy! Five'll get you ten there's a *gun* in that bag of hers and she sleeps with it under her pillow!"

"Knock it off, Teddy!" snapped Iris.

"By the way, Howie, have they missed that case of stuff you lifted from the cannery yet? I found it under the bed in the room you just vacated."

Howard might have been frothing at the mouth when he said, "What kind of a crack is that, Soberjowski? And since when is it a crime for a supervisor to bring home samples?"

Teddy abruptly changed course. "How are things at the hospital, Doc?"

Silence followed, and I guessed that Doc was engaging in *his* favorite pastime (gazing at Patsy, whose place was directly across the table from his own). "Doc? . . . Hey, DOC!"

The clatter of silverware landing on the bare wood floor could only mean that Doc had come to with a jerk, knocking half his place setting off the table. I had seen it happen before. Sometimes he tipped over his water glass, too. Poor lovesick Doc!

"What? . . . Oh. I'm sorry?"

Patsy rescued him with a gentle, "I think Teddy was asking about the polio count, Doc."

"Oh, the polio count! . . . It's bad and getting worse,

I'm afraid." *It sent a shiver down my back to hear Doc say they'd had five new cases in two weeks. And we were barely into July!* Patsy asked whether there would ever be a vaccine for polio and Doc said, sure, researchers were working on it right now, but it could be years—maybe even decades—before we finally had one.

Mrs. Mumson had finished spearing potatoes in the oven with a long-handled fork and arranging them on a platter around the biggest rib roast I had ever seen. Instructing me to bring the gravy and the side dishes, she hefted the large platter with difficulty and carried it into the dining room.

There were gasps, followed by "oohs" and "ahhs" from the table.

"Judas Priest, Mums!" shouted Iris. "Is the war over?"

Declaring that it must be 110 degrees in the kitchen (what a day to have the oven on for hours!), Mrs. Mumson delivered the platter to the table where a wicked-looking set of carving knives was waiting.

Margaret asked where in the world it had come from, such an enormous cut of meat, and Mrs. Mumson said, "Well, you'll have to ask Teddy about that, Margaret. All I know is, after I said wouldn't it be nice to have something special for our Fourth of July dinner, he brought me this!"

Still in the kitchen, I was pouring gravy from the enameled baking pan into a china gravy boat when I heard Howard remark, "Say, I'd like to meet that Miss

Kitchen at the paper who dreams up the stuff the *kid's* been cooking! Would I give *her* a piece of my mind!"

"You can't spare any," said Teddy dryly.

Patsy weighed in with, "What's the prob, Howard? It's all good healthy stuff. Take those bell peppers stuffed with rice and peanuts we had the other night."

"I'd rather not," snorted Howard. "But they weren't as bad as those curried oysters."

Iris put in her two cents' worth: It was the baked bean sandwiches in her lunch box. And then, in her shy way, Margaret said it was the prunes in everything. And they all agreed it was the *prunes!*

I paused in the transfer of the gravy and tried to remember what it was that Miss Kitchen said prunes added to today's meatless meals. I did use a lot of them, it was true, but so what? *Miss Kitchen wouldn't give you a bum steer!*

After a moment I heard Howard say, "Well, Mumsy? Aren't you going to tell us where you got that big roast?" But Mrs. Mumson repeated what she had said earlier, about asking Teddy. It was all his doing, don't you know.

Howard saw a chance to make trouble for his old roommate. "The papers are full of stories about the meat shortage in Sacramento, Soberjowski. I'm not eating a bite of this until I know where you got it!"

Patsy tried to head him off. "What's the diff, Howard? Maybe he got it at the racetrack. Stop looking a gift horse in the mouth, if you get what I mean!" but Teddy swore it wasn't horse meat.

Iris was suddenly agitated. "Maybe it's black market beef!"

"Keep your shirt on, Iris," snapped Teddy. Then he explained that a guy owed him a favor, see? The guy happened to be a butcher and he had this nice big roast that he was saving for another customer. "It took a little arm-twisting, but he sold it to me instead."

At that moment I pushed open the swinging door and carried in a tray holding the brimming gravy boat and serving dishes piled high with vegetables.

"You can ask Smitty! She was there. Weren't you, Slugger?"

"Huh?" (I was concentrating on keeping the tray level so the dishes of vegetables wouldn't slide off. Any wobbling, and the gravy would go over the side of the gravy boat, too.)

When it was all safely down on the sideboard Teddy asked me to tell the gang what we did yesterday.

"Oh! Teddy's got a new car."

Howard exploded. "Another new car . . . !"

"It's a beaut!" I said, sounding more like Patsy the hep cat every day. "We went for a spin with the top down!"

"Yeah, but where did we go?"

"You mean, to get the roast?" I was starting the side dishes around the table. "We went to Shultz's Market."

Mrs. Mumson looked up from her carving job.

"Why, I've been trading at Shultz's Market for years. Really, Howard, what could be wrong with that?"

"Nothing, *if* they gave the butcher enough red stamps for it!"

Teddy said, "Tell him, Smitty."

"Boy, I'll say we did! A good roast beef costs twelve points a pound now. But I've saved so many stamps with Miss Kitchen recipes, we could afford it."

Teddy grinned. "Enjoy it while you can, boys and girls. Tomorrow it's back to soybeans!"

"Oh, no. Not tomorrow. Tomorrow I'm gonna try 'You-Know-Whose' recipe for braised cabbage, ham hocks, and *prunes!*" Then I retreated to the kitchen, just ahead of a collective groan from around the table.

A moment passed before I heard Margaret say that they all owed Teddy—not only an apology—but a vote of thanks for the feast.

Patsy agreed. "Margaret's right. Thanks a heap, Teddy!" and Teddy said, "Okay, folks. Dig in."

And they did. The clatter of silverware against Mrs. Mumson's good bone china was evidence of that.

In the kitchen I fixed myself a small plate and sat down in the breakfast nook, next to an open window. Voices continued to drift in through the gap in the swinging door.

"Mmmm. It's been so long since I've had real meat I've forgotten what it tastes like!" declared Patsy.

Iris (who had been silent since her theory of black market beef had been shot down) said, "You'll get plenty of it in the WAVES. We civilians have to make sacrifices so that our fighting men and women—"

But she was cut off in mid-sentence by Doc, who coughed loudly and took a gulp of water before he said, "The WAVES? Are you going into the WAVES?" and Patsy told him about taking Japanese to see if she could qualify for the Navy's interpreter program.

Although no one had asked, Howard declared that *he* would join up in a minute if his job at the cannery wasn't classified "Essential." Then he crowed, "But the war'll be over before they'd call me and the rest of the 2-Cs!"

Teddy said, "Don't break your arm patting yourself on the back."

Doc, who was still thinking about Patsy (*what else was new?*), said he might be joining up, too. That got the predictable response from Mrs. Mumson. "Oh, Doc! Don't tell me I'm going to lose both of you?"

Doc said the papers were saying that ten thousand doctors would be called up this year alone. Then he added shyly that since he wasn't a father . . . or even married . . . he felt it his duty to go.

Teddy couldn't resist saying, "Well, heck, we can fix that, can't we, Patsy?" and Patsy told him tersely to shut his trap.

Howard was still itching for a fight. "And what about you, Soberjowski? How come Uncle Sam hasn't called you yet? What kind of a deferment have you got, anyways? Or, are you one of those draft dodgers we hear so much about?"

Teddy said simply, "Can it, Howie."

But Howard persisted. "Iris says you've probably been in the service already and got a 'bad conduct' discharge. Maybe for black marketeering."

Teddy said, "Thanks a lot, Iris. I'm crazy about you, too!"

Mrs. Mumson felt it was time to intervene. "Oh, Howard! Teddy! Can't we have a little peace for once? This is a holiday, after all!" Then she declared that Teddy's deferment—if he had one—was nobody's business but his own.

Teddy said he didn't mind telling Bird Brain that his draft status was 2-A, if that would shut him up.

Howard scoffed, "*Two-A?* You know what that means? It means the used car business is essential to the national health and safety, *that's* what it means!"

"Howard, please!" scolded Mrs. Mumson.

"*Two-A?* Don't make me laugh!"

"Pipe down, will you, Howard?" Now it was Patsy doing the scolding. "Mumsy's right. This is a holiday. And God only knows where any of us will be, or what we'll be doing, on the *next* Fourth of July!"

Margaret's "Yes, God only knows" was barely audible, but Teddy's response came out loud and clear. "That's right! Y'know, times like *these* are about as unpredictable as boardinghouse stew!" (I was sure Mrs. Mumson was about to react to the hated word "boardinghouse," but Teddy still had the floor.) "Assuming the war's not over yet, Doc and Patsy will be off somewhere in the service. Howie'll still be canning peaches, and Iris will still be bullying the neighbors during the black-outs. What about you, Magpie? What d'you think you'll be doing?"

Margaret began to stammer, but she was interrupted by Mrs. Mumson's, "Oh, dear! We're missing Walter Winchell."

Mrs. Mumson never missed Walter Winchell. Next to Mr. Anthony at the famed Marriage Institute, he was her favorite.

I could hear the old radio crackling to life. A moment later, Walter Winchell gave his first "Flash!" Betty Grable had married bandleader Harry James that day in Las Vegas. Controlling the hep cats had been a problem for police. Betty and Harry had made a movie together last fall, and that was the end of Betty's long-time boyfriend, George Raft!

His second "Flash!" was about Mrs. Roosevelt's comments over reports of promiscuity among WAACS and WAVES. She had said it was only *German propaganda* that America's servicewomen would be issued contraceptives! The society column of the *Washington Post* had declared recently that (quote) sex had reared its ugly head in the WAACS and WAVES (unquote)!

Mrs. Mumson gasped, "Mercy!" and turned the radio volume down when Walter Winchell said he would return after a word from his sponsor. "I do hope that's not true about sex rearing its ugly head in the WAACS and WAVES," she lamented. "Oh, it's this

war! Before Pearl Harbor young women were expected
to behave like ladies. But now that girls are being called
on to do almost everything *boys* do, why, morality's
gone out the window!"

Iris guffawed, *"Ladies* in the WAACS and WAVES?
Flora Mumson, you are a case!"

Howard asked Patsy if she knew what W.A.V.E.S.
stood for, and Patsy said, "Sure. It stands for Women
Appointed for Voluntary Emergency Service," and
Howard said with a snicker, "Wrong! It stands for
Women Are Very Essential Sometimes!"

"Strictly off the cob, Howie," groaned Teddy.

Mrs. Mumson turned up the volume on the radio
again. A "Flash!" from Walter Winchell reported on
the number of Japanese now in relocation centers—
110,000—but some 1,000 each week were being discharged to settle inland, away from the western
coastline. His next "Flash" told of a new wonder drug,
called penicillin, which was being used to treat war
wounds and gonorrhea. It was made from green mold!

After that, Walter Winchell concluded with his usual,
"And that, ladies and gentlemen, winds up another edi-
tion of the Jergens Journal. Until next week at the very
same time—and with 'lotions of love'—I remain your
New York correspondent . . ." but today being the Fourth
of July, he added that every American should feel fortu-
nate that we still salute a *flag* and not a *shirt!*

Now it was time to dish up my crowning achieve-
ment of the day, a special Fourth of July dessert.

CHAPTER SIX

DANCING IN THE DARK

I was humming "The Stars and Stripes Forever" as I carried my tray into the dining room on a wave of patriotic pride. There were seven delicate sherbet glasses on the tray, each with a serving of my fabulous Fourth of July creation. Setting the tray carefully down on the sideboard, I proceeded around the table, picking up dirty dinner plates and passing out dessert spoons.

Patsy was standing in front of the old radio, impatiently twisting the big brown knob. "What this party needs is music to give it a little oomph!"

Teddy said she should try and get Artie Shaw. He was supposed to be playing at the Triannon Ballroom. My John Philip Souza was soon drowned out by Artie Shaw and his "Back Bay Shuffle" as I went around the table dealing out sherbet glasses.

Patsy said, "Hey, glom this everybody! Smitty's made us a red, white, and blue dessert!"

"For Pete's sake, don't ask her what's *in* it!" Howard warned sharply.

I was crushed. I stuck out my lower lip and whined, "Gee, it's only three flavors of ice cream . . ."

Mrs. Mumson was the first to come to my aid. "Yes, Howard," she chided, "Eileen has been cranking my old ice cream freezer all afternoon, making this lovely dessert. And in this terrible heat, too!"

I had retreated, pouting, to my kitchen when I heard Margaret saying softly, "That wasn't very nice, Howard," and Howard responding defensively, "Well, how was I supposed to know it was something *normal* like ice cream?"

Doc told Mrs. Mumson it wasn't good for me to work so hard, especially in this hot weather. He said he'd seen me coming from the store on my bicycle several days that week with heavy loads of groceries in the basket. (Patsy interjected, "It's all those bottles of Clorox!" which I knew was directed at Iris.)

Doc went on to say, "After all, Mumsy, Eileen is still a little girl."

Uh-oh! Did Doc know I was only eleven years old that summer—not "going on thirteen" like I told Mrs. Mumson? A pediatrician, even an intern, would know stuff like that, wouldn't he? And if he knew, would he tell?

I held my breath. But it was Margaret's voice I heard next, agreeing with Doc that I was doing too much. Imagine her surprise, she said, when she came down to get a glass of milk at six o'clock one morning and found me on my hands and knees, scrubbing the kitchen floor!

Well, it wouldn't surprise my father. Remember that "fastidious gene" I was supposed to have inherited from him? Anyway, who did they think would do the heavy cleaning if I didn't? I couldn't see Mrs. Mumson down on her knees! So with Janet in the shipyard and Yukie—the Japanese gardener and houseboy—behind barbed wire, there was no one but me. *The only game in town, my father would say.*

Back in the dining room Patsy was reminding every-one that Janet used to clean the bathroom once a week. "But Smitty cleans it every day!"

"And shines Howie's shoes, too," growled Teddy.

Howard countered with, "So? She still has time to go out joy riding with you, doesn't she?"

You could tell Mrs. Mumson was really trying to find a solution to the problem of my being overworked (and one that wouldn't cost her anything). "Doc may be right about the groceries being too heavy," she con-ceded at last. "I'll tell her to make more trips and carry a lighter load each time."

Teddy called her a "female Simon Legree," and added, "Don't worry, Doc! From now on I'm taking the kid shopping in my *car!*"

"The Lone Ranger to the rescue," sneered Howard. "Hi ho Silver!"

At the end of the summer I would recall those words and understand why, as I waited for the smart comeback that would put Howard in his place, Teddy said noth-ing. *Howard thought he'd won that round, I guess.*

Teddy was humming along with the music on the radio and Howard baited him with, "One of your *people*, isn't he, Soberjowski? Artie Shaw, I mean."

"Yeah! His real name's Arshawsky. Bet you didn't know that, did ya, Bird Brain?"

Howard dismissed that with a "Hmph!"

"Listen! This is a good jump tune. Come on, Patsy. Kick off your shoes and let's show these tin ears how to cut a rug!"

"And ruin my only pair of nylons? Don't be ridic!"

"How 'bout you, Magpie? You wearing nylons, too?"

Margaret started to stammer, the way she always did when she was nervous. "N-n-no, but I . . . I don't know how, Teddy. I n-n-never learned."

By that time I was over my pout. I went back into the dining room to gather up the dessert dishes.

Teddy was snapping his fingers and swaying to the music, a lively Artie Shaw favorite called "Cross Your Heart." More as a joke than a serious question, he called out, "Hey, Slugger! You don't jitterbug, by any chance?"

"Sure! My sister's in high school and she teaches me all the latest steps!"

Teddy's face registered momentary surprise, then broke into that radiant grin that made me fall in love with him the first time I saw it. Holding out his arms to me he said, "Well, come to Papa!"

In an instant I was somewhere out in space—or maybe on the moon! I felt weightless and giddy. Teddy held me in his powerful grip, swinging me first to one side and then the other across his knees, then up over his head and down nearly to the floor. Miraculously, each time he set me down I landed upright and never missed a beat. We went "truckin' on down," we did "the Shorty George," and every other step I knew, and some I didn't. Like all really good dancers, Teddy could lead. And I could have followed him with my eyes shut!

With everyone scrambling to get out of our way, we spun once around the dining room, then through the wide archway into the parlor (where there was more room to dance), and back again.

At the end of that number, the band swung into "Dancing in the Dark," and so we collapsed, out of breath and laughing, into the big leather armchairs. Our performance was applauded by all but Howard (who thought dancing was sinful), and Mrs. Mumson, who looked shocked. "Gracious," she gasped, "what kind of a dance did you say that was?"

"The jitterbug, Mumsy," panted Teddy, "but if you want to try it, you'll have to wait 'til I catch my breath!" A moment later he jumped up, grabbed my hand, and said, "Your sister teach you to fox trot, too?" and I said, "Nope. I taught *her!*"

And so, for the next few minutes I was Ginger Rogers, in a pink-and-white-striped pinafore, and Teddy was Fred Astaire, as we glided around the floor to the haunting melody of "Dancing in the Dark."

To say that I was in heaven would be a gross understatement.

The piercing wail of a siren brought an abrupt end to Artie Shaw—nee Arshawsky—and dancing with Teddy on that most glorious Fourth of July.

❖ ❖ ❖

Iris was swinging into action with all the bravado you would expect from a "Home Front Commando." She tossed the canvas bag over her shoulder, strapped the white Civil Defense helmet under her chin, and blew shrilly on a silver whistle that hung around her neck on a braided cord. As if the rest of us were stone deaf, she shouted, "Air raid siren! Blackout! All right, Mumson, you know what to do!" Mrs. Mumson wasn't so sure she *did* know what to do, and an exasperated Iris yelled, "The blackout curtains! Pull 'em *down!*"

Patsy pointed out that it was hardly even dark yet, and Teddy said it could be a false alarm. It was a new system and someone might have made a mistake.

But Iris would tolerate no dissension in the ranks. "You want me to write you a citation, Soberjowski? I want those curtains down! And kill that radio!"

Teddy gave a shrug and went to help Mrs. Mumson pull the ominous black curtains down over the tall windows.

Iris raced toward the steps leading to the front hall but turned and barked her final orders before charging out, like Teddy Roosevelt up San Juan Hill. "I've got to see that other houses on the block are blacked out! Everybody else stay inside! Close these doors behind me. And remember, when you hear a one-minute blast, it'll mean the 'all-clear!'"

Doc got up and shut the french doors behind Iris and closed off the parlor, too, where there were no blackout curtains.

More or less marooned together in the stifling dining room, we waited, listening for the "all-clear."

Margaret broke the silence with a timid, "What if it r-r-really is an air raid?"

Patsy told her to relax. No one would *dare* bomb this country on the Fourth of July! Not if they knew what was good for them.

I went to turn off the lights in the kitchen, and Howard said he might have left one on in Iris's (soon to be his) room. He went upstairs to check, ignoring Teddy's suggestion that he should leave it on and make Iris write *herself* a citation.

Doc, who had spent most of the previous night at the hospital, sat down wearily and said he hoped the alert would be over soon. He needed to get back again.

Patsy said, "You really care about those kids, don't you, Doc?"

Running a hand through his thick red hair, Doc said it would fairly break her heart to see some of them. "I just hope I live to see a world where children grow up with no threat of polio, smallpox, or even measles!"

"Or war, either?"

"Right! No war, either."

I had brought what was left of the ice cream to the

table and noticed that Doc might actually be on the verge of a breakthrough in his perpetually stalled romance with Patsy. Switching my attention for a moment (the wrong moment, as it turned out) to check on Patsy's reaction, I didn't see Doc abruptly pushing his chair back, just as I passed behind it. There was a loud "thump!" as we collided, and the ice cream cylinder flew out of my hands and rolled under the table.

Doc was mortified. "Oh, gosh! I'm sorry! My fault! . . . Here, let me get it, Eileen," and he went down on all fours and crawled under the table after the retreating freezer can.

Teddy sighed, "Doc, you're a klutz. I sure hope you're not planning to be a brain surgeon!"

Doc handed me the container before crawling out from under the table and bumping his head in the process.

Teddy rubbed his hands together and said with a devilish grin, "Anybody for a game of cards? Or spin the bottle? Blackouts can be fun, you know!"

Patsy said pointedly that she would get the *cards*, and opened a drawer in the sideboard.

I started around the table again, offering more ice cream.

"I'll have some, Slugger," said Teddy, and Patsy said she would, too. When Margaret said she'd like another scoop, Mrs. Mumson said she was glad to see her getting her appetite back again—and putting on a few pounds, too, or she'd miss her guess!

Margaret's normally colorless face suddenly looked flushed, and she tugged at her white middy blouse.

Patsy was shuffling the cards. "What'll it be? Poker?" She looked up and saw Howard coming in through the french doors. "What about you, Howard? You wanna play?"

Howard scowled at her and ignored the question, so Teddy said, "Holy Rollers don't play cards, Patsy."

That got Howard's goat. In three giant steps he was standing beside Teddy's chair, with his fists clenched. "I've had just about enough of your remarks," he said angrily.

Slowly, Teddy stood up. Now they were toe to toe, glaring at each other. *Howard was a little taller, but when Teddy clenched his fists, too, you could see the muscles bulging in his arm. I was sure that Howard would get the worst of it in a fight. Even so, I was plenty scared!*

Mrs. Mumson tried to defuse an explosive situation by scolding both of them in the strongest terms yet. "Boys!" she said sharply. "I'm ashamed of you, acting like a couple of hoodlums! Sit down, Teddy! You, too, Howard!"

Looking like prizefighters being told to go to their respective corners, Teddy sat down again and Howard grudgingly went around the table to his place and sat down. (Mrs. Mumson's seating chart had wisely put them on opposite sides.)

Patsy was still calmly shuffling the cards. *You'd have thought she'd been someplace else while all this was going on!* Taking right up where she left off, she said, "How about you, Margaret? You want to play?"

Margaret shot Howard a quick glance before saying, no, she didn't think so.

"Doc?"

Doc was looking at his watch and seemed about to decline, but Teddy said, "Aw, come on, Doc. What's that old saying? 'Unlucky at love, lucky at cards?'"

The next sound we heard was not the "all-clear," but the telephone ringing in the hall. Mrs. Mumson slipped out to answer it, and I took the empty ice cream container back into the shadowy kitchen.

I heard Teddy, Patsy, and Doc beginning to play cards at the table. They were talking loudly and laughing. Patsy couldn't get over it—Doc was holding four aces! And Teddy said, "Didn't I tell you he'd be lucky at cards?"

Another conversation, this one between Margaret and Howard, was taking place right on the other side of the kitchen door from where I stood at the sink.

"Howard, we have to talk."

"Shh! They'll hear you."

"But we need to decide something. Soon!"

"Well, are you really sure, Margaret? I mean, couldn't you have made a mistake?"

"I'm as s-s-sure as I can be."

"Look, we can't talk here. We'll meet tomorrow. At the usual place."

I wished with all my heart that I was not hearing this intensely private conversation. I thought of pushing open the swinging door and saying, "Oh! I didn't know you were there!" But it was too late. Margaret was crying softly.

"Don't cry, for Pete's sake! It's going to be all right. We'll do . . . something."

"*What*, Howard?"

"I don't know yet."

"We can't wait much longer. Everyone will know! Even Mumsy noticed that I'd gained weight!"

"Listen, Margaret, it's the worst possible time. I'm in line for a big promotion at the cannery!"

"Howard, the telephone company has a very strict policy about . . . this kind of thing. I'd be fired in a minute!"

Outside the blacked-out windows of Mrs. Mumson's boardinghouse the wail of a siren announced the "all-clear." And inside one thing was "all clear" to me, now. *And I wished it wasn't!*

I waited until I was sure Margaret and Howard had moved away from the swinging door before going back into the dining room. Mrs. Mumson was just coming in from the hall (she must have been on the telephone the whole time). "Oh! Is that the 'all-clear?'"

Teddy said, "Yeah. Let's get these curtains up and the windows open. It must be close to a hundred in this room!"

Doc got up from the table, saying he guessed it was

safe for him to leave, now that the blackout was over. As he headed for the french doors, still looking back at Patsy, he said, "It was fun, though, playing cards." Then, "Oops!" as he tripped over a chair.

Teddy deadpanned, "It's only a matter of time 'til Doc breaks a leg. Then we'll have to shoot him."

I sneaked a quick look at Margaret. She was wiping her face with a linen handkerchief, pretending it was the heat. But her large, mousy brown eyes were still filled with tears.

"So, who was on the phone, Mumsy?" asked Patsy.

Mrs. Mumson said excitedly that it was long distance. Her son-in-law had just taken Jenny to the hospital! By this time tomorrow she reckoned she would be a grandmother!

Patsy said, "Congrats!"

Mrs. Mumson clasped her pudgy hands and squealed, "Oh, I just love babies, don't you?"

I was ready for the sharp look that passed between Howard and Margaret, but Mrs. Mumson never noticed. (Apparently she had forgotten her initial worry about Margaret's possibly being "in a family way.") She had other things on her mind now. "But, oh, dear! It means I have to leave right away."

Patsy told her not to worry about her "guests." They'd be in good hands with little Miss Kitchen here! And by the way, the ice cream was delish! Surveying the melted remains of all three colors in her bowl, she tried to place the flavors. The white part was easy. That was vanilla.

And there was the blueberry. But what about the red? Didn't taste like strawberry or cherry . . . What was it?

"Beets," I said matter-of-factly.

There was dead silence after that. *You could even hear the clock ticking in the kitchen!*

"Well, gee," I began, sensing that I'd better make this good, "I didn't have any of those other things—strawberries or cherries—and the store's closed today, so I . . . well, we've got some swell little beets in the Victory garden now, and my aunt makes beet *wine,* so I thought, why can't you make beet ice cream?"

A whole minute ticked by before anyone said anything. Then Teddy smiled weakly and offered a measure of support. "Sure, why not? It's, uh, y'know, not bad at all!"

Howard moaned, "I *told* you not to ask her what was in it!"

I was spared further reviews of my latest culinary creation by the noisy return of Iris, who announced that she had only got halfway around the block before the "all-clear" sounded. "But I caught that dizzy dame across the street with her shades up!"

Teddy said, "Bully for you, Iris!"

Some movement outside the window suddenly caught my eye. Nearly screaming, I said, "There's somebody out there! He was looking in the window!"

Teddy jumped up and ran past me to the window, demanding to know who. What did he look like?

"Like a Chinese, or—"

But it was Iris who finished my sentence. "A Jap! I told you this could happen! They've landed! RIGHT HERE IN SACRAMENTO!"

And I watched in horror as she yanked a pistol out of her canvas bag.

CHAPTER SEVEN

MEETING YUKIE

The last few minutes had seemed like a nightmare; one where I'm staring down the barrel of a big ugly gun. Worse than that, Iris was holding it!

Teddy and Howard had rushed out the back door, hoping to catch whoever it was that I had seen looking in the window. Moments later we heard shouts and sounds of a scuffle coming from the general direction of the kitchen, then the swinging door flew open. We all froze as Teddy and Doc, one on each side, dragged an Oriental boy into the dining room. Howard followed a few steps behind.

He was tall for an Oriental, but his rumpled clothes hung loosely on a gaunt frame. His face was smudged with dirt, his straight black hair a tangle of weeds and sweat. He stared open-mouthed at Iris and the gun pointing at him.

"Well, here's our Peeping Tom!" announced Teddy.

Doc explained that he was just going out the front

door when he heard a commotion around back, "and we caught this young fellow trying to break in!"

They were still holding the struggling boy by his arms when he said, "No! Honest, Mrs. Mumson! I was just about to knock when they jumped me!"

Iris was waving the gun excitedly. "Okay, I got this one covered! How many more are there?"

Mrs. Mumson, who had finally noticed what Iris was doing, said with alarm, "Iris! Where did you get that awful gun?"

Teddy took a step toward Iris, dragging the boy along with him. "You numbskull! Put that thing away before somebody gets hurt! Can't you see he's just a kid?"

Doc was looking curiously at their trembling captive. "Wait a minute. What did you say, son?"

"I was just trying to tell Mrs. Mumson that I wasn't breaking in!"

Recognition suddenly broke over Mrs. Mumson's astonished face, and she exclaimed, "Why! As I live and breathe! It's Yukie Matsumoto!"

Howard said, "I don't get it. You mean you know this little Nip?" and Mrs. Mumson explained that he used to work for her, as a houseboy and gardener.

Teddy loosened his iron grip on Yukie's arm and said, "Hope we didn't hurt ya, kid," and Doc let go of the boy's other arm, saying he guessed they had all jumped to the wrong conclusion.

Only Iris was left to point out the obvious. *Obvious to her, anyhow!* "Not so fast! He's still an escaped prisoner of war!"

Teddy told Iris if she didn't put that damn gun away he'd come over there and ram it down her throat! *And Mrs. Mumson didn't even scold him for swearing!*

Doc, the voice of reason in this tense little drama, said calmly, "Let's hear what the boy has to say."

But Iris, who was like a bulldog when she got her teeth into something, was not one to listen to reason. Still waving the gun, she yelled, "How do we know what he was doing out there, during the blackout? Maybe he was signaling enemy planes!"

Yukie was looking more frightened with each passing minute, but now I saw something besides fear in his eyes. It was hunger. The boy was hungry, maybe even starving!

Teddy dropped Yukie's arm and took a few steps toward Iris and the gun. "I'm warning you, Iris!" he said fiercely. "Put that thing down!"

Left unsupported, the boy swayed and then crumpled in a heap on the floor. Teddy helped Doc lift him up and sit him in a chair. When he opened his eyes again, Doc asked him when he had eaten last, and Yukie said he thought it was yesterday, or maybe the day before. He wasn't sure.

Compassionate Patsy murmured, "Poor kid!" and asked Mrs. Mumson if we couldn't at least give him a bite to eat. And the lady of the house (who was not without a heart when the chips were down), said she didn't see why not, and instructed me to run out to the kitchen and fix him something. I thought about the remains of the big roast cooling on the platter under the kitchen window. Could I make him a sandwich with that? One look at Yukie's glazed eyes and Mrs. Mumson said decisively, "Yes, yes dear! And you'd better hurry!"

I bounded out through the swinging door and was soon cutting thick slices of brown bread, ready to pile them high with slabs of roast beef, lettuce, tomato, and whatever else was at hand. Meanwhile, Iris was saying, "Mumson! Are you crazy? Roast beef for a J—" but Teddy cut her off with a warning that she'd better shut her big mouth or he would shut it *for* her.

Doc said, "I don't see any harm in feeding a hungry boy."

"Fine!" snorted Iris. "And if the emperor drops in, we'll serve tea!"

Teddy said that wasn't a bad idea, but let's make it coffee. (That was too much for Iris. "*Coffee . . . !*") "You heard me. How 'bout one of you girls putting it on, while Smitty's making the kid a sandwich?"

Margaret volunteered to do it. She was halfway through the swinging door when Teddy called to her, "And make it strong, Magpie. None of that watered-down 'Victory coffee' today!"

Alone together in the cavernous kitchen, Margaret and I went about our separate tasks—she filling the big blue enameled pot with water and asking where I kept the coffee, and I setting about building a sandwich that would satisfy a ravenous Dagwood Bumstead. At some point it occurred to me that there might be a silver lining in all of this: Yukie's dilemma was now the focus of our attention. (*Not that you could forget for one minute that you were in "a family way!"*)

I put the sandwich on a tray with a tall glass of milk. For dessert I added a dish of my Sugarless Prune Whip (which Miss Kitchen had touted as a good way to use leftover prunes) surrounded by crisp peanut butter cookies.

Pushing open the swinging door with my shoulder, I backed into the dining room with Yukie's tray. Mrs. Mumson was still adrift about that day's surprising turn of events. "I can't get over it! We never expected to see *you* here, Yukie! Not until the end of the war, anyway." And after a moment's reflection, "Just what *were* you doing out there in the yard?"

"He was spying on us!" Iris was sure of that.

Howard offered, "The war's not over, as far as we know, so either he was released for some reason or—"

"I ran away!"

"You mean escaped!" Iris corrected him. "From the concentration camp!"

Yukie allowed that when you were a prisoner there it might *seem* like a concentration camp. "But they call it a relocation center."

I set the food on the table in front of Yukie, who

marveled, "Wow! Is that real? I can't remember when I've had roast beef!"

Iris still had the gun in her hand, but she leaned forward and rested it on the table while she fixed Yukie in her steely gaze. "We hear you get a lot of things *we* don't! Everything's rationed for *us*, y'know!"

Yukie was attacking his sandwich like the Starving Armenians our mothers told us about (*who would eat your vegetables, and anything else you left on your plate, and be glad to get it*), but he paused long enough to say, "Oh, we've got rationing in the camp, too! And there's a shortage of just about everything except the stuff we grow ourselves."

"That ain't the way I heard it!" Iris insisted stubbornly.

Margaret came back into the dining room. "Coffee should be ready soon."

Patsy had an idea. "Maybe we ought to pull these shades down again. We don't want the neighbors in on this, do we?" Teddy agreed, and together they lowered the blackout curtains for the second time.

There was something intrinsically depressing about wartime blackout curtains, and the events of this day only added to their air of impending doom. As soon as the curtains were down, I switched on the Tiffany-style leaded glass lamp over the dining room table, which threw colored light in the shape of fruits and flowers against the dull black fabric of the curtains. But even that did little to dispel the gloom.

Suddenly becoming alarmed, Iris protested. "Wait a minute! This begins to have all the earmarks of harboring a criminal!" With that she started off toward the front hall, with the telephone as her objective. "I'm calling the FBI!"

"Not so fast, Iris." Teddy had blocked her path so quickly that Iris took an awkward step backward in surprise.

Howard said suspiciously, "What's your objection to calling in the law, Soberjowski?" and Iris chimed in with, "Yeah! Maybe *you* don't want the feds nosing around, for some reason. Maybe *you've* got something to hide!"

It was Mrs. Mumson who settled the matter. Raising her voice above the bickering, she said, "You all seem to be forgetting that this is my house! When I think we need the authorities, I'll call them!" She had put her foot down and seemed to feel all the better for it.

In the next instant there was a loud hissing noise from the kitchen that made us all jump. Margaret gasped, "Oh! The c-c-c-coffee! It's boiling over!"

"Never mind, Margaret," Doc said. "I'll get it."

Mrs. Mumson took a dainty handkerchief out of her sleeve and wiped her damp forehead. "We're all a good deal overwrought, I'm afraid. And before this war is over, we'll all be mad as hatters!"

The sandwich, milk, and cookies had disappeared as if by magic from Yukie's tray, but the dish of Sugarless Prune Whip remained untouched. (*I wondered what the Starving Armenians would do with that.*)

Yukie was apologizing to Mrs. Mumson. He hadn't meant to cause her any trouble. "When I jumped off that truck I didn't know where I was going or what I was going to do. I didn't even think about coming here, at first. I just wanted to get away!"

"You say you jumped off a truck?" asked Teddy. "Where was that?"

"Out in the Valley. They brought us down to work in the sugar beet fields."

"Brought you down from where?" Howard wanted to know.

"A place called Tulelake. Up near the Oregon border."

Doc came in, holding the silver coffee urn a safe distance from his shirt front with two hot pads. Teddy sniffed the steam emanating from the pot. "Ah! Smells good. And with all due respect to Mrs. Roosevelt, I'm going to have some. Anyone else?"

Mrs. Mumson said she would have a cup, and added defiantly, "With three lumps of sugar in it, too!"

I filled the cups and passed the sugar and cream, and everyone—except Iris, who used the occasion to bemoan the lack of patriotic spirit in this house—had a cup of coffee. Even Yukie had one, which only added insult to Iris's injury.

Patsy sat down next to Yukie. "You say you were sent to Tulelake? Why not the camp at Manzanar?"

Yukie said Tulelake was where they sent most of the farmers, but added, "My dad wasn't really a farmer, y'know. He was more like a florist. He grew flowers in our little place in the country and sold them in his shop here in town."

"But we heard you went east, someplace."

"Well, that was the first time. My dad gave up the shop and moved us to my uncle's farm. It's outside the 'restricted' zone, and he thought we'd be okay there. They told us we wouldn't have to move again, but a couple of months later they rounded us *all* up—my uncle, too—and took us to Tanforan."

Mrs. Mumson thought she remembered that Tanforan had something to do with horses or something, and Teddy said, "That's right. It's a racetrack. Just south of Frisco."

Patsy asked how long he was there, at Tanforan, and Yukie said about four months.

That gave Mrs. Mumson a jolt. "Heavens! You were living at a racetrack for four months?"

For the first time since his unceremonious arrival, Yukie smiled. "You might not call it 'living,' Mrs. Mumson," he said wryly.

Margaret said, in her shy way, that she had heard conditions there were "shameful," and Doc said he had heard the health care facilities were almost nil. The smile faded from Yukie's face as he muttered, "Yeah. You said it!"

Iris rolled her eyes and threw up her hands in mock exasperation. "Well, maybe we should've put 'em up at the Ritz, with room service and—" but Teddy cut her off with, "Iris? You wanna wake up in Palookaville, you just keep on beatin' your gums!"

Iris crossed her arms over her wrinkled khaki shirt and went back to sulking. But I noticed (with some relief) that the gun was left lying on the table, just out of her reach.

"Go on, Yukie," prompted Patsy. "You were telling us about Tanforan."

A thought dawned on me as Yukie was talking. *Why, he was every bit as American as I was!* "As American as apple pie" *were words I had heard in a movie once. Mrs. Mumson had said Yukie was a citizen, just like the rest of us. I tried to put myself in his place: being as* "American as apple pie" *and still having your country lock you up—not for anything you did, but for what someone, somewhere, thought you might do!—And now, those same people wouldn't be happy 'til they locked up the Germans, too!*

"It wasn't so bad for the kids," Yukie was saying. "Some of the littler ones thought it was okay. Kind of like camping out. I guess the worst thing for me was having to leave my dog behind. No pets allowed. But it was a lot worse for the grownups. They had to leave just about everything behind!"

Yukie paused long enough to ask Mrs. Mumson if she thought she could spare another glass of milk. Without waiting for her answer, I snatched up the glass and hurried out to the kitchen with it. *I didn't want to miss a minute of Yukie's story!* When I returned, he had just started telling about what they could—and couldn't—take with them into the camps.

"See, we only got to take what we could carry. Just our clothes, personal stuff, and bedding. But no mattresses. They gave us those when we got there." Then he corrected himself. "Well, not mattresses, exactly. They gave us big pillowcases and told us to stuff them with straw." He smiled again as he said, "That night, when we went to bed, some of us joked about 'hitting the hay!'"

Margaret asked where they slept, and Yukie said, "In the stables. One family to a stall."

Mrs. Mumson gasped, "Mercy! You slept in a stable?" to which Iris sang out, "It was good enough for Jesus Christ!"

Dead silence followed. Everyone was staring at Iris, too embarrassed to say anything. I sneaked a look at Yukie, who seemed strangely unfazed by Iris's tasteless remark. *He was probably used to people saying dumb things!*

Finally, Teddy shook his head and said, "I swear, Iris, you've got more nerve than a sore tooth!"

Patsy urged Yukie to go on and just ignore what *anybody* said. But she was glaring at Iris when she said it.

"Well, the first night in the stables, the floor was covered with manure."

That got Howard's attention ("Howard is very fussy about practically everything," Mrs. Mumson had said on my first day here), and he wrinkled his nose and said with disgust, "Sleeping in a barn with manure! That . . . that's *unsanitary!*"

Yukie continued, "The whole place was guarded by soldiers. With machine guns! They searched us for knives and razors when we first came in. I guess they thought we'd try to cut our throats or something."

Instinctively, my hand went up to my throat, and I couldn't help trying to recall what kind of razor my father brought to our house on his infrequent visits. Then I could see it, lying on the glass shelf above the bathroom sink. *One of those scary things that opened up like a jackknife! I shuddered, just thinking about it.*

Patsy was asking how many people were there, at Tanforan, and Yukie said he didn't know for sure. "We heard rumors, though. In the camp there are rumors about everything—you name it. One time we heard there were about fifteen thousand of us." Then, in a bemused afterthought he added, "Fifteen thousand is a lot of people at a racetrack, even when the ponies are running!"

Mrs. Mumson could hardly take it all in: Such inhuman conditions!

"My mom couldn't get over the lack of privacy. Like the public showers."

Iris, in another bold display of ignorance, remarked that she thought "his people" *always* bathed together, and I could have hugged Yukie when he reminded her that "his people" were Americans!

Mrs. Mumson weighed in at that point, and with some degree of irritation in her voice. "I told you before, Iris, Yukie is an American citizen—war or no war!" Her tone softened as she turned back to Yukie and said, "Go on, dear."

"Well, things got better after a while. We built furniture and planted gardens. Vegetables, and even flowers."

Patsy guessed what came next. "And so, natch, they moved you again."

"How'd you guess?"

"It figures."

When they got to Tulelake they had to start all over again. There, the camp was nothing but Army barracks and bare dirt with barbed wire around it.

"But at least we had a room, even if it was only twenty by twenty . . . Well, we really had *half* a room. Each one had to hold two families. But we had cots, and there were stoves, too! . . . A big improvement over the stables!"

Margaret was the first to say what most of us were thinking: "Two families in a twenty-by-twenty room? That's criminal!"

Doc said it was a wonder there wasn't more disease. And just think about mothers trying to manage families under such conditions!

Yukie agreed it was tough, all right. A look of pain darkened his face when he said, "And besides, my mother was sick. We knew something was wrong while we were still at Tanforan, but up at Tulelake she got worse. When she finally got to see a doctor they said it was cancer. They operated, but . . ." He turned to the gentle redhead with the stethoscope jammed in his pocket. "it was like *you* said. About the health care facilities? They were so bad! The hospital didn't even have enough nurses. My mom was always getting up and taking care of someone who was worse off than she was." Then his voice trailed away to a whisper. "Two weeks later . . . she died."

At that moment everything seemed to stop in the overheated room with the gloomy curtains and too many sweating bodies crowded together inside. A stunned silence hung in the air, like the last toll of a church bell after a funeral. No one moved. No one said anything. Then a loud sob into the folds of Mrs. Mumson's handkerchief broke the silence. A rush of words went around the room, murmured condolences for the sorrowful boy who had lost so much—his home, his mother, even his freedom.

"What can I say?" asked Patsy, hugging Yukie's thin shoulders. Looking around helplessly at the rest of us, "What can anyone say?" No one answered.

Even Iris had been moved by the boy's story, to the extent that some of her icy resentment was melting away. Without a word she scooped up the gun from the table and shoved it back into her canvas bag.

Obviously not used to being on the receiving end of sympathy from his fellow Americans, Yukie at first seemed overwhelmed. Tears made rivulets through the smudges on his face."My dad didn't even have any flowers for my mom's funeral! He'd been a florist most of his life, and now he had no flowers for his own wife's funeral!" Then, wiping his face on his sleeve, he said, "Gee, I . . . I'm sorry."

Mrs. Mumson was wiping away her own tears. "You go ahead and cry, dear, if it makes you feel better."

But Yukie seemed determined to go on, to get it all out. Life was uncertain, at best, for the people in the camps. It crossed my mind that he thought there might never be another opportunity to say these things.

"It was like the family just kind of fell apart after Mom died. My dad had some sort of a stroke or something. Now he just sits and stares at the floor. My sisters have to take care of him, just like a baby." And as if that wasn't bad enough, he added, "My brother's turned into a Kibei!"

Patsy looked puzzled. "A Kibei? I thought that was a Nisei who'd gone back to Japan."

Yukie nodded. "That's right. But in the camps we use it to describe a guy that acts 'Japanesy.' They're real troublemakers. And there's a rumor that Tulelake will get all the Kibei from the other camps. A kind of 'segregation center for disloyals.' Boy! Things'll be *really* bad then!"

Margaret said it wasn't hard to see why Yukie had run away, and Patsy said, "Check! But what happens now?"

The question was directed at Teddy. For it was Teddy who spoke with the real voice of authority in the house, though at the time none of us could have said why, exactly. And despite anticipating the answer, it was no easier to accept.

"He'll have to go back."

Margaret inhaled sharply. "Oh, Teddy!"

"Can't be helped, Magpie. But the whole family might be out soon, anyway."

It nettled Howard anytime Teddy appeared to have inside information, and this was one of those times. "How do you know so much about it?" he growled.

"Howie, even a dope like you can keep his ears open. Didn't you hear Walter Winchell say that about a thousand a week are being discharged from the camps, to settle inland? Having a sick father should hurry things along, too."

Mrs. Mumson patted Yukie's hand. "There, now, dear. You see? Things aren't so bad, after all!" Thus satisfied that Yukie's troubles were practically over, she ventured, "But does he have to go back right away, Teddy? As long as he's *here*, don't you know, couldn't he stay long enough to prune the camellias?"

Teddy gave her a long, exasperated look, but said nothing. *And I knew why. What he was thinking couldn't be said in Mrs. Mumson's presence!*

Yukie said with alarm, "You're going to send me back?"

"Look, kid, don't be a sap," Teddy said, as gently as an older brother might instruct a younger one in the wicked ways of the world. "You can't walk around the streets of

Sacramento. This is still a restricted zone. The FBI would pick you up inside of a week."

Doc asked Yukie again where he had jumped off the truck that brought him down from Tulelake, and Yukie answered, "Someplace out in the Valley." Then he added, "But it's not there now. They were planning to head north again last night. Or this morning, for sure."

Teddy was shaking his head. "We'd never catch it. Not even in my souped-up Roadmaster! We'll have to think of some other way to get him back to the camp."

Mrs. Mumson frowned and said, "But if he can't even walk around the streets of Sacramento, Teddy, how in the world is he going to travel?"

In the funny papers when someone has a bright idea, a light bulb goes on over his head. I saw one now, over Teddy's head.

"With you, Mumsy!"

"With me? How? I don't understand."

But Patsy did. "I get it! . . . Mumsy's going up north to be with her daughter—"

Now Doc got it, too. "And Yukie can go with her."

"Right. And they'll be taking the 'scenic route' through Tulelake!"

Trust Howard to throw cold water on any plan that had Teddy's fingerprints on it! "Well, pardon me for living, but how's he supposed to get on a train without anyone noticing?"

It was Margaret who answered simply, "He'll be wearing a disguise, of course."

The next problem, what kind? I didn't know how it would help, but I repeated what I had said when I first saw Yukie through the window: That he might be Chinese.

Patsy gushed, "That's it! We'll disguise him as Mumsy's *Chinese maid!*" and Margaret added, "With a hat and veil."

Yukie took exception to the idea of dressing him in women's clothes, but no one was listening. Teddy was asking Mrs. Mumson how soon she could leave, and after a moment's hesitation, she said, "Why, tomorrow if necessary."

"Good! I'll make your train reservations. Yukie should get to Tulelake about the same time that truck does."

Margaret frowned and said, "But, Teddy, suppose he gets to Tulelake all right. He can't just walk back into the camp, surely. How will he get inside?"

"Leave the details to me, Magpie."

That rankled Howard, the way it always did when Teddy seemed to have something up his sleeve, a mysterious power to accomplish things that no one else could. Take the way he had come home with a roast the size of a bread box, saying a guy owed him a favor! And now, being able to sneak a fugitive back into a secure government installation!

"Another guy 'owes you a favor,' I suppose."

"Now you're gettin' smart, Howie!"

Patsy thought of something else. "Wait a sec. If we

put him in a dress, what happens when he has to go to the little boys' room on the train?"

Howard grinned. "Yeah! Answer *that* one, Mr. Anthony!"

But Teddy, as usual, was out in front of the pack. "Simple. We get Mumsy a private compartment. After all, a lady traveling with a maid would go first class, wouldn't she?"

That satisfied Patsy, if not Howard. "Bingo! . . . Well, I can't think of anything else, can you, Margaret?"

Margaret said no, but turned to the Elephant in the Room. "You haven't told us what *you* think, Iris . . ."

Iris declared that as long as he went back—and the sooner the better!—she guessed it was okay with her.

Now, with everyone on board, it was time to put the plan into action. Mrs. Mumson said she had a full evening's packing to do, and Patsy and Margaret put their heads together about proper duds for her "maid." Margaret offered a hat with a full veil, and Patsy said fitting Yukie into a skirt—and shoes!—would be the next prob.

In the center of the storm was Yukie, who was walking a fine line. "I know you're all trying to help me, and I appreciate it. Honest! . . . But—"

Doc knew what was on the boy's mind. "We can understand why you don't want to go back, son. But Teddy's right. It's the only thing to do."

Patsy gave Yukie's shoulder another squeeze. "It's too bad, honey. But it's a *shikata ga nai!* Correct?"

Yukie looked blank and said, "It's a . . . what?" and Patsy explained that, literally translated, she thought *shikata ga nai* meant a "can't be helped thing." Wasn't that right?

Yukie said he didn't know. He never learned Japanese. "My dad wouldn't allow it. He wanted his kids to be one hundred percent *American!*"

Another loud sniff into her soggy handkerchief from Mrs. Mumson summed up the feelings of the majority in the room: What could he have been *thinking*, our President Roosevelt, when he signed Executive Order Number 9066, authorizing the internment of Japanese-Americans, regardless of citizenship? And closer to home, our own Governor Earl Warren—later chief justice of the Supreme Court? How could this great country, this great state, treat its own people so *badly?*

CHAPTER EIGHT

PULLING TOGETHER

It was well past midnight before any of the "conspira-tors" in the plot to return Yukie to the camp at Tulelake finally doused the lights and went to bed. All evening the rooms belonging to Patsy, Margaret, and Mrs. Mumson had resembled nothing so much as a busy sorority house. Voices, footsteps, and the sounds of frantic activity floated down to me in the kitchen. Preparations were proceeding on schedule for tomor-row's departure of Mrs. Mumson and her "Chinese maid."

Yukie, for the first time in a year or more—and pos-sibly the last time, too, for a while—had enjoyed a good hot bath and gone to sleep between clean white sheets in a real bed with a thick mattress and plump feather pillows. (He was in Howard's old bed in Teddy's room.)

With the last of my chores finally finished, I tumbled into my own bed in the little room off the kitchen, only to toss and turn without sleeping. My mind kept going back over the events of the day, and

I was worried. Not about Yukie. I had complete confidence in Teddy's ability to get the boy safely back into the camp ("Leave the details to me," he had said with a wink and a grin).

No, Yukie was practically home free. Well, as "free" as you can get and still be a prisoner! It was Margaret I was worried about.

Since coming to work at the boardinghouse (was it only five weeks ago?), I had grown fond of Margaret. She was a gentle soul, and vulnerable, too, just as Mrs. Mumson had said. The more I knew about her situation, the more I worried about what she might be driven to do. *I shivered, remembering Shirley Connor's sister!*

Mrs. Mumson had observed that "morality's gone right out the window," because of the war. And to people of her generation it must have seemed so. Boys were going off to fight, girls were being left behind, and no one knew what the future held for any of them. ("Times like these are about as unpredictable as boardinghouse stew," Teddy had joked.) A whole generation of young people was finding itself caught in a shifting tide of moral behavior. Nevertheless, a girl still trembled at the thought of bearing a child out of wedlock.

And that's the way Margaret was trembling now.

Shirley Connor was a girl in my class at school. Like me, she had an older sister. One day Shirley came to school and told some of her friends that her sister had been arrested. We all listened in rapt attention to the gruesome tale, as Shirley (who was none too bright, herself) told about how her dumb sister had "borned" a baby in the bathroom the night before, wrapped it in newspaper, and thrown it in the trash can behind their house. The girl had thought the baby was dead, but sometime during the night it began to cry. That alerted the neighbors. One of them remembered seeing a girl, whom he could identify, dumping a newspaper-wrapped bundle into the same trash can where the infant was found by police some hours later. But the baby was premature, and too small (even Shirley's mother did not suspect her older daughter of being pregnant!) to survive on its own. Leaving her child to die in that manner was called a crime of shocking cruelty. Shirley's sister was sent to prison.

The grandfather clock in the front hall chimed twice. I was drifting in and out of a troubled sleep when I heard another sound. The old staircase had one squeaky tread and when the house was quiet you could always tell when someone was going up or down the stairs. Then it squeaked again. Two people. And coming down.

Maybe it was Margaret heading to the kitchen for a glass of milk, as she often did at odd hours. But who was with her?

The door to my little room next to the pantry was ajar and I could just make out two figures coming through the swinging door from the dining room. Then, in the dim moonlight filtering through the tree outside my window, I could see her. She was crying and gripping what looked like a shoe box in her trembling hands.

Now Howard was beside her, supporting her by one arm as they made their way through the shadowy kitchen to the back door.

I couldn't breathe. I prayed that I was having a nightmare and would wake up and find that what had seemed so real was only a bad dream. And so I waited there in the dark, wanting to scream but unable to make a sound. Minutes, maybe hours, dragged by.

The moon slowly disappeared and dawn finally broke outside the window. I was mentally and physically exhausted, but I knew I had better get up and start breakfast, no matter what grizzly event had or had not taken place in the night.

Later, as I stood at the stove pouring pancake batter onto a hot griddle, I began to question my own judgment about what I had (or had not?) witnessed. Nothing out of the ordinary seemed to be happening upstairs. The sounds that filtered down to the kitchen were no different from those of any other morning. And I was fairly certain, from the number of doors I heard opening and closing, that Mrs. Mumson and her six "guests" (plus one extra in Teddy's room) were all present and accounted for.

By eight o'clock it still seemed like a perfectly normal morning, except for some extra activity surrounding Yukie and Mrs. Mumson. A platter of protein-rich

Cottage Cheese Pancakes was keeping warm in the oven, along with two pounds of crisp bacon (at five red stamps per pound). I had forced myself to keep busy by cooking a huge breakfast. Now there was nothing to do but wait.

As soon as I heard people descending the stairs, I peeked out through the gap in the swinging door to watch for Margaret. When at last she appeared, I sighed with relief to see that she looked no thinner today than yesterday.

So Margaret and Howard and baby-makes-three were still intact after all.

After breakfast Teddy took Mrs. Mumson and Yukie to the train station in his latest and snazziest car yet, the "souped-up Roadmaster," a shiny, midnight-blue Buick heavy with chrome and "power to burn." (*The way Teddy drove those hot cars of his almost scared me to death a couple of times. Today I was keeping my fingers crossed that he would take it easy and not get pulled over for speeding. And him with a fugitive in the back seat!*)

The rest of us had peered out of windows to watch Yukie taking his first cautious steps in a pair of blue and white spectator pumps. We all agreed that in Patsy's clothes he did make quite a convincing "girl." She had put makeup on him, too, over his strenuous objections. But whether or not you would take him for Chinese would depend on your knowledge of Asian features. Luckily, his face was mostly hidden behind Margaret's black hat with the heavy veil.

❖ ❖ ❖

With Mrs. Mumson gone, things began to change in the boardinghouse, although less so for me. I had the same amount of work to do, except for one less bed to make (hers) and one less person to wait on. But it was obvious that house rules were falling by the wayside, with no one to enforce them and scold offenders. Swear words crept into everyday conversations. People began to smoke in the parlor and dining room without regard to the prohibition against it. Under Mrs. Mumson's watchful eye smoking was permitted only in a boarder's own room. Now Iris had taken to chain-smoking at the table!

All summer it had been almost too hot to go outside—not that it was any cooler in the house. But the Victory garden would not take care of itself.

So-called Victory gardens had begun springing up everywhere and in some of the most unlikely places during the war years. Right here, in the middle of a major city, little plots of vegetables had replaced all or parts of people's lawns and flowerbeds. Growing your own food was the patriotic thing to do. *How is this different from picking tomatoes out in the Valley?* I asked myself, wiping sweat out of my eyes on a scorching hot day in the garden.

From the position of the sun that afternoon I could tell it was time to go in and put my casserole (a new Miss Kitchen recipe) in the oven for our early Sunday dinner. It was more like a late lunch, really. As a rule, Mrs. Mumson did not serve dinner on Sundays.

As I bent over the hose to wash the garden soil off my hands, I had the oddest sensation. The ground was coming up to meet me! I felt dizzy and my head ached, so I sat down on the splintery back steps and rested for a minute before going into the house.

Teddy was on the telephone in the hall when I went through the swinging door to the dining room. The dizziness returned while I was setting the table. I had trouble focusing my eyes, and my mind seemed to be playing tricks on me.

Through a strange buzzing in my ears I heard Teddy talking to the operator. "I want to make a person-to-person call to New York City. And reverse the charges, will you, sweetheart?" (*Now, what did I do with the water pitcher? I had it in my hand a minute ago. At least I think I did!*)

"Hello, New York? I want to speak to a Mrs. Hubbard at Murray Hill 26503 . . . That's right." (*Who's Mrs. Hubbard? Never heard Teddy mention anyone by that name before.*)

"My name? Ranger. And make it snappy, will ya?" (*Ranger? Did he say his name was Ranger?*)

"Hello, Mother Hubbard? . . . Yeah, Lone Ranger. I got your message. What's up? . . . Okay. Name? . . . How do you spell that? . . . Got an address? Hold on a minute, Mother. I gotta get this down." Teddy was scribbling in a notebook. (*Mother Hubbard? Lone*

Ranger? What kind of a game was he playing? And where the heck was that water pitcher?)

"Okay, shoot . . . Description? . . . What color is 'hazel?' . . . Oh, green. What's he driving? . . . Cadillac, huh? That ought to raise some hackles around here. One guy in particular is pretty nosy about the cars." (*That would be Howard. And if Teddy's got a Cadillac coming, Howard will be plenty sore about it! Now, was I looking for the cream pitcher or the water pitcher? I must be going crazy.*)

"I have to hang up now, Mother. I'm in a boardinghouse. Too many people around." (*Yes, and little pitchers have big ears!*) "You'll get the usual message soon as I find the guy . . . Right."

Teddy hung up the phone and went up the stairs, two at a time.

My head was throbbing and the buzzing, like the sound made by the old radio, was getting louder. *I was wishing with all my heart that Christian Scientists would let you take aspirin!* When Doc came down to lunch I would ask him if he had anything for a headache that my mother would approve of, though that seemed highly unlikely. And where was Doc, anyway? He hadn't shown up for breakfast, which meant he was probably at the hospital. I would just have to suffer.

Back in the kitchen, I was gathering up a stack of plates and only dimly aware of the front door being opened and slammed shut. Unbeknown to me, Iris had entered with several large Army/Navy Store bags,

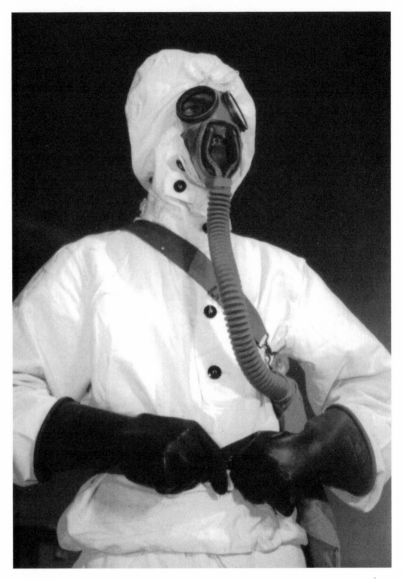

A serviceman looking like a space alien in a gas mask.
Library of Congress Collection.

which she carried into the dining room and dropped on the floor next to the table. The bags contained the promised gas masks—hideous looking things with big goggle eyes and air hoses like small elephant trunks. Naturally, Iris was eager to try one on.

The stack of plates was heavy and required two hands to carry, so I pushed open the swinging door with my shoulder and backed into the dining room. When I turned around I faced a terrifying, unearthly apparition. My mind reeled, unable to cope with all the strange things that were happening today. *Mother Hubbard! Lone Ranger! And now a creature from outer space!*

I couldn't help it. I began to scream. Not a little "eeeek" as if I had seen a mouse. More like "Aaaggghhh!"—shrill enough to shatter glass and loud enough to be heard in Lodi. A second later the heavy stack of plates hit the bare wood floor with a sickening crash.

My reaction so unnerved the "creature" that it rushed toward me, waving its arms and trying to shout something from inside the horrible mask. All I heard were muffled alien sounds as I was being chased around the table.

My hysterical state made it obvious, even to Iris, that she had better ditch the offending mask if we were ever going to have peace in the house. So she started struggling with the buckles that held it tight against her head. But they would not budge.

The Western Pacific Exposition Flyer.
Courtesy the California State Railroad Museum.

By now my screams had been heard by everyone in the house, if not every house on the block. Teddy was first on the scene. I saw him racing down the stairs (as my father would have said), like the Exposition Flyer on a downhill grade and three hours behind schedule!

Bolting across the dining room he reached out and swept me into his arms.

"Smitty, it's okay! It's only Iris, honey. See?" Then he turned on my alien tormentor. "For Christ's sweet sake, Iris! Haven't you got anything better to do than go around scaring little girls? What the hell are you playin' at? This ain't Halloween!"

Teddy was hugging me to his chest. He had been dressing to go out at the moment my screams had brought him unexpectedly back downstairs, in his lightweight tan jacket, white shirt, and blue slacks. And now I had a new worry: Why was Teddy wearing a shoulder holster?

There was no mistaking it. I had seen enough gangster movies to know a shoulder holster when I saw (or felt) one. I suddenly remembered what Mrs. Mumson had said on my first morning here: "We don't really know *what* Teddy does. We just hope it isn't anything illegal!"

Was Teddy a gangster? And what did Mother Hubbard have to do with it? He had hung up the phone after talking to her and gone right upstairs to dress before going out. *And now he was packing a rod!*

Patsy ran into the dining room, with a wide-eyed Margaret close behind. "Holy Toledo!" Patsy gasped, catching sight of Iris. "What's going on? Is there a gas attack?" and Margaret screamed, "Gas! . . . We're all going to d-d-die!"

Iris was still struggling with the straps, so Teddy reached over the top of her head and yanked the mask down over her face, leaving it dangling a few inches below her chin.

"Hey! Just pull my whole *head* off, why don't you?"

"Don't *tempt* me!" And Teddy gave one of the Army/Navy Store bags a vicious kick. "Now get this crap outta here!"

"Iris, when are you going to quit playing stupid *war games?*" Patsy chided. Then, focusing her attention on me, she said, "You poor kid. You're all flushed."

"I don't feel good, either. My head hurts."

"Come and sit down, then." And turning to Margaret, "Help me crack a couple of these windows, okay?"

I was still keeping a wary eye on Iris, half expecting her to turn back into an alien. She and Teddy were glaring at each other across the jumble of bags on the floor. Finally Iris stuffed the offensive mask back into a bag, scooped up all the bags, and stalked out, passing Howard on his way in.

"What's all the commotion? What's going on down here, anyways?"

Teddy said he wasn't sure, but he'd bet that Iris had come in looking like something out of a Pathe newsreel and scared me out of my wits. Then he pointed to the clutter of broken dishes on the floor. "We better get this mess cleaned up."

Howard was staring at the carnage. "Wow! Is Mumsy going to be mad when she comes back and finds half her plates busted!"

I had forgotten all about the dishes. Now I stared at them, too, and began to wail all over again.

"Now see what you've done, Bird Brain!" stormed

Teddy. "Make yourself useful for a change, will ya? Go get the broom!"

"Well, you don't have to get sore," Howard grumbled. "Where is it?"

"Where's *what?*"

"The broom. How am I supposed to know where she keeps the broom?"

"I'll get it," I said through wrenching sobs. But I hadn't taken two steps before I felt my knees turning to jelly. The room started to spin and then something like the blackout curtains fell all around me, and it was very dark inside.

❖　❖　❖

I must have have been semiconscious for the next few minutes. Although I couldn't open my eyes, I was aware that Teddy had caught me before I hit the floor and now I felt myself being lifted up and carried to the window seat. Voices, sounding very far away and anxious, drifted in through the darkness. First Patsy's "She's fainted!" then Margaret's hysterical "What's the *m-m-matter* with her?" and Teddy's "It's all that damned Iris's fault! I oughtta wring her neck!" And Margaret again, "Look how red her face is. She must be feverish!" I felt Patsy's soft hand on my forehead. "She *is* feverish! Hot as a fire-cracker!" and Teddy was asking, "Where's Doc?"

Patsy thought Doc might be upstairs sleeping. He'd been at the hospital all night. Teddy told her to go and see if he was in his room. And if he was, to get him down here "on the double" and tell him to bring his bag with him! Patsy's heels went clicking away across the floor and Teddy called after her, "If he's not there, get the car keys off my bureau. We'll take her to the hospital!"

Uh-oh. My mother wouldn't like that!

I could hear Patsy running up the stairs, calling "Doc! . . . Doc!" and Margaret standing close to me, murmuring, "Teddy? Do you think it's . . . ?" But she couldn't say what was on everyone's mind—*including mine!*

Teddy said nothing, but I felt his cool hand smoothing the damp hair away from my face.

"Remember what Doc said to her that morning?" That was Howard. "If you feel like you have a fever or a bad headache—" and Margaret said it was obvious that I had a fever, and I had just told them I had a headache! Then Howard said it (what was on everyone's mind): "Doc told us he had six new cases of polio at the hospital just this week!"

I drifted away into the blackness. Then, in the distance I heard the sound of bare feet running down the stairs, with Patsy's high heels close behind. And now Doc was kneeling beside me. I heard the click that his black bag made when he opened it.

"How long has she been out?" Doc was asking in a new, professional voice I had never heard before. Teddy estimated the time at two or three minutes. "Has she opened her eyes at all, since then?" No, Teddy said.

Then Doc spoke to Patsy. The voice was still professional, but with a softer tone. "Patsy, would you go into the parlor and get some cushions and pillows off the sofa, please? Oh, and that knitted what-do-you-call it."

"The afghan?"

"That's the one."

Margaret said she would go too, and both girls hurried off in the direction of the parlor.

I heard Doc rummaging in his bag for something. "Okay, young lady, we're going to try and wake you up now." He was cracking something open and then waving it under my nose. "That's a girl! Come on. Wake up." *One or two whiffs of that stuff and I was awake, all right!*

Now that I could open my eyes I looked up at all the anxious faces staring down at me. Margaret and Patsy were holding armloads of things from the parlor and waiting for further orders from Doc. "We'll spread the cushions along the window seat under her, and prop her head up with the pillows." Teddy and Howard lifted me up while the cushions and pillows were put in place. "That's right. Now cover her with the afghan."

Everyone seemed to recognize and respect Doc's authority in the present situation. He was clearly the man in charge, and my admiration for him grew by leaps and bounds. I wondered what Patsy thought. Was she seeing him, for the first time, as a perfectly competent physician—a world apart from the sad clown who was always falling down and breaking things?

Doc was shaking a thermometer and telling me to put it under my tongue.

I started to say something but he had said not to, so I didn't. (*I wanted to ask him what polio felt like when you had it.*) He was busy taking my pulse when Patsy said, "Doc? Is it, you know . . . ?" and he didn't answer right away. As if to himself, he said, "Pulse is a little fast. Could be just the excitement."

Almost unnoticed, Iris had wandered in through the french doors. "What's going on? Somebody sick?"

Teddy blocked her progress toward the window seat. "Back off, Dozier. She sees *your* ugly puss, the kid could have a relapse!"

Doc was saying, "Okay, Eileen, let's see if you can move your arms and legs. Does that hurt? . . . Don't talk, just nod or shake your head . . . Any stiffness? How about your neck? . . . No?" Looking around at the others he asked what had brought this episode on. Did anyone know?

Iris was still being held at bay by Teddy, but managed to say that she had come in with our gas masks, see, and put one on. Just to see how it fit, and all. "And she got scared," she concluded with a shrug of her shoulders. Teddy said it was because she looked like a freakin' commando! (*I wanted to say she looked more like a spaceman, but I had the thermometer in my mouth.*)

Doc stood up for the first time since I had opened my eyes, and I got a look at what he was wearing. It was obvious that Patsy had rousted him out of bed in a hurry. He had come downstairs in a cotton robe loosely thrown over a pair of striped pajamas. He was barefoot and his hair resembled a bird's nest made of twisted red twigs. He looked like a little boy on Christmas morning, only taller and needing a shave.

Turning to face the group, Doc said, "Will one of you get her a glass of water? And let's have some ice and a towel—unless someone has an ice bag."

As if the director had shouted "Action!" on a busy movie set, people rushed off in every direction. Teddy and Howard tripped over each other getting to the table and snatching glasses of water to hand to Doc. Patsy and Margaret swept out through the swinging door, saying, "I'll get some ice," and "I'll get a clean dish towel." Even Iris got into the act. "I think there's an ice bag up in the bathroom!" and she loped out through the french doors.

I was beginning to think Doc had forgotten about the thermometer, but at last he took it out and studied it for a moment. Again, as if talking to himself, he said, "Her temperature's 102, which isn't too bad for a youngster." *It sounded pretty bad to me!* Kneeling beside me again, he said, "Now let's have a look at your throat. Open wide and say 'aaaaah.' Uh-huh. Never had your tonsils out, have you?" I shook my head, even though I could talk now. He was opening a bottle of white tablets. "I want you to take two of these with plenty of water."

This was not the time to tell him about my mother being a Christian Scientist, *and what my mother didn't know wouldn't hurt her, either!* So I swallowed my guilt along with the tablets.

Margaret and Patsy returned from the kitchen with a big chunk of ice in a pan and some dish towels. Iris came back in, waving an old gray ice bag. Doc began filling it with ice that Patsy chipped out of the pan with an ice pick.

Finally he turned to the assembled faces, all looking strained and worried. "I'm pretty sure it isn't polio."

That triggered a collective sigh and a torrent of words, all spoken at once and tumbling over each other.

Margaret said, "Oh! Thank goodness!" and Teddy said, "Jesus, that's a relief!" and Howard said, "It sure is! Polio's contagious, isn't it?" and Iris answered, "Yeah!" and Patsy asked, "But if it isn't polio, Doc, what is it?"

"A combination of things. Exhaustion, for one. I warned Mumsy about letting her work so hard, particularly in this hot weather. She's dehydrated. Also, her tonsils are inflamed. They should have been taken out before this." (*Try telling that to my mother!*) "And maybe a touch of sunstroke!"

"*Sunstroke!*" gasped Margaret.

As if he had forgotten that I was awake now, Doc asked the others what I'd been doing today. Did anyone know? Margaret told him I had been working in the Victory garden, and Doc said, "I thought so. Well, she's got to take it very easy for a while." Then he asked if anyone had heard from Mrs. Mumson. Iris said she'd had a letter yesterday, but it didn't say anything about coming home any time soon.

Teddy was outraged. "Oh, yeah? Well, I'm sending her a wire right now!" On his way to the telephone, he turned back to Iris and asked, "What's her daughter's address?"

Iris volunteered to get it for him, and the two of them marched out together (*together!*) into the hall and up the stairs.

Patsy pursed her lips, today a lustrous strawberry that matched her sweater. "From now on, I'm going to clean my own room!" Then, sternly addressing the rest of the group, "And we can *all* help with the cooking!"

To everyone's surprise, Howard was the next to volunteer. "I'll take over the Victory garden." We all stared at him, not sure we had heard correctly. "Well, what's wrong with that?" he asked defensively. "I come from a farm, y'know!"

Sniffing the air, Margaret said, "Do I smell something burning?"

It suddenly occurred to me that my casserole had been in the oven—for how long? It would be completely ruined by now. I struggled to get up from the improvised bed on the window seat, but couldn't seem to get my feet under me. Then Doc's hand was on my shoulder and he was telling me to stay where I was. He wanted me to rest a while and keep the ice bag on my head.

"And don't worry about dinner. We'll look after it," vowed Margaret. She and Patsy disappeared through the swinging door.

Teddy was on the telephone in the hall. "Hello, operator? Get me Western Union . . . Yeah, I'll wait." I could just see him if I peeked out between Doc and Howard and, as I expected, he was down to the white shirt and blue slacks. His tan jacket (and the shoulder holster, presumably) had been left in his room when he went upstairs with Iris.

Iris came back in and asked, "Where's Margaret and Patsy?" Howard said they were in the kitchen seeing about supper, and Iris grabbed him by the collar and said, "Well, come on, Dillingham. I'm putting *you* on k.p.," and she dragged him out through the swinging door.

At the same moment, Margaret came in, holding a smoking pan out in front of her. "What's this?" she asked, wrinkling her nose. "Or rather, what *was* it?"

I stared at the remains of my new Miss Kitchen recipe for low-point meats: Liver Potato Puff, but sensed that Margaret did not share my disappointment that it was ruined. In fact, she looked relieved as she wheeled around and took the blackened pan back to the kitchen.

As Margaret went out, Patsy came in. "Have we got plenty of eggs, Smitty? Howard's going to make us a Denver Omelet." I told her there was a full dozen in the cooler. Patsy went out as Iris came in. (*You could get dizzy just watching that door swinging back and forth!*)

"Where's the big copper kettle? I'm gonna start some spaghetti sauce for tomorrow." I said it was next to the big frying pan in the pantry, just as Howard stuck his head in. "Hey, kid, where's a big frying pan?" Iris pushed him back out, saying, "She just told you! Next to the copper kettle in the pantry!"

Doc was putting things back into his bag. Teddy hung up the phone in the hall and strode into the dining room, looking well pleased with himself. "Wait 'til Mumsy sees the wire I sent her! It'll curl her hair!" And approaching the window seat, he said, "How're you doing, Slugger?"

I had to confess that I was worried about what was going on in the kitchen. "I better go see what they're doing out there." But when I tried to get up, the room tilted sideways. Doc said he wanted me to stay down. "Try to take a little nap."

I was feeling sleepy, all right. I wondered what was in those pills.

❖   ❖   ❖

I was drifting into a peaceful sleep when Teddy suddenly said, "Listen, Doc! Did you hear that?" Then he leaned over me and threw open wide the window above my head. "Sounds like an 'Extra' on the street!" And now I could hear what Teddy was hearing: a newsboy calling "Extra! Extra! Read all about it! . . . Italy surrenders! Italy surrenders! . . . Read all about it—"

Teddy gave a shrill whistle. "Hey, *kid!* Over here! Give us a paper, Sonny." He tossed a coin out the window and brought in a paper. "Keep the change." The boy said, "Gee, thanks, mister!" Then he went away again, calling, "Extra! Extra!"

Teddy unfolded the newspaper. "Wow! Take a look at this, Doc! 'Italy surrenders. General Marshall Says War is in Final Stages!' How 'bout that?"

Doc called to the others in the kitchen. "Patsy! All of you! Come and look at this!"

First Patsy, then Margaret, Iris, and Howard filed in through the swinging door, each wanting to know what all the excitement was about.

Teddy waved the newspaper and crowed, "Italy's surrendered! That means one down and two to go!"

Howard grabbed the paper out of Teddy's hand and repeated, "'War is in Final Stages!' Hey, everybody, this calls for a celebration!" Trotting out through the french doors, he said, "Pardon me while I go up and get some stuff from my room." Then, halfway up the stairs, "Are we gonna eat good tonight!"

Teddy watched him with mock amazement. "What? Howie breaking out the booty from under his bed? Now that *does* call for a celebration! And I've got a bottle of French Champagne I've been saving. I'll go get it."

Patsy said okay, but make it snappy. Dinner would be ready in a jiff.

Teddy said he'd be back in a flash and bounded up the stairs in his usual fashion, two at a time.

Patsy turned to Doc and asked if he was ready for something to eat, too. She was smiling her all-American-girl smile and you could see Doc's heart melting. The bright blue eyes weren't sad now! Doc and Patsy stood beaming at each other, and I felt a certain pride in helping to break the ice for them. *If it took me getting sick before those two could get together, well, maybe it was worth it!*

But the Fates, as usual, were against them.

It was obvious that since his emergency call to the dining room, Doc had given no thought at all to what he was wearing. Now he looked down at the wrinkled pajamas and loose cotton robe, and his face began to color. In a return to his usual persona, he stammered, "Oh! I'm sorry. I'm not dressed!"

He was backing toward the french doors, clutching the robe around him, when Patsy said, "Wait a minute! Here's your bag, Doc."

"Oh, yes. Thanks," Doc said, swiftly returning to the spot where he had left the bag and stooping to pick it up. Unfortunately, Patsy had done the same thing, and at the same time. I closed my eyes, not wanting to see what would happen next. But I heard it. Like two stags in mating season, their heads came together with a resounding "Thwack!" When I opened my eyes, both Doc and Patsy were looking dazed and rubbing their heads.

Doc said, "Oh! I'm terribly sorry! Did I hurt you? I've got an awfully hard head." And Patsy said, "Boy! You're telling *me!*. . . No, I'm okay. I think."

Doc stayed long enough to say, "Are you sure? Well, I'll go upstairs and change. Won't be long!" Then he fled through the french doors, tripping over the hall carpet before ascending the stairs on the run.

Margaret had watched this fresh disaster from a quiet corner in the dining room. Coming closer to Patsy, who was still rubbing her head, she asked timidly, "What's his problem, anyway?"

Patsy said it wasn't really Doc's fault. Everything just seemed to go all haywire between them!

Margaret thought a minute before lamenting, "Well, Patsy, if a girl like *you* can't get her man, I guess there's no hope for the rest of us!"

Patsy moaned, "It seems like every time he gets within ten feet of me he *breaks* something. Ooooh! This time I think it was my skull!" Reaching for my ice bag, she said, "Can I borrow this?" and planted it on her own head.

Iris was still reading the newspaper, and Patsy asked how long she figured the war would last, now that Italy had surrendered. But Iris scoffed, "Don't count your nylons yet, Patsy! Italy was a walk around the block, compared to Japan and Germany."

The mention of Germany pulled me back from the brink of sleep, and I mumbled (I had trouble forming the words), "I saw a sign on a telephone pole downtown. 'Now that we got the Japs out of California, let's get the Germans out, too!' it said."

Patsy and Margaret both rushed to reassure me.

Patsy with, "Now, honey, don't start worrying about that again," and Margaret with, "Yes. You hush, now. Doc said you have to rest."

Before closing my eyes (they were getting so heavy!) I saw Patsy look sharply at Margaret, then heard her say, "You ought to get a little rest yourself, Margaret. You look fagged. Are you okay?"

Margaret's answer was anything but convincing. "I . . . I'm all right," she said softly.

Iris abruptly slammed the newspaper down on the table. "Uh-oh! I think Howard left his omelet on the stove!" And she bolted out through the swinging door.

Next, I heard Howard coming down the stairs and saw, through half-closed eyes, that he was carrying a large cardboard box. "Yes, sir. We're going to eat good tonight!" He sounded almost gleeful, which was quite out of character for Howard (and as if he didn't have a care in the world, I thought sourly).

Teddy followed, coming through the french doors clutching a bottle of wine. After Howard was safely out of earshot, he said, "Imagine Major Hoople sharing all that hoarded loot with us! And look! He even gave me a cigar. Can you beat that? Holy Howie passing out cigars. You'd think he was having a baby or something!"

My eyes flew open, just in time to see Margaret react with a start.

Teddy was uncorking the bottle. "Real French Champagne, girls! Sorry it's not cold. We'll have to put ice in it." He poured several glasses and added some chips from the block of ice that had filled my ice bag (the one Patsy was now wearing).

"Hey! This reminds me of a movie I saw the other night. Listen. Who's this?" Then Teddy said in a growly voice, "You played it for her, you can play it for me. Play it, Sam! . . . Well?"

Patsy said it was John Garfield, and Margaret guessed Ronald Coleman, but I said Humphrey Bogart (only it came out "Bumfry Hogart") and Teddy raised his glass and said, "Here's lookin' at *you*, kid!"

Just then Iris stuck her head through the kitchen door and announced dinner. ("COME AN' GET IT!" she bellowed.)

Margaret, Teddy, and Patsy filed out. Patsy turned back halfway through the swinging door and said, "You stay put, Smitty. I'll bring you a plate in a sec."

I knew I would be too groggy to eat anything, but I smiled and nodded my head, anyway. As I closed my eyes again waves of laughter and animated conversation began flowing from the kitchen—sounds more associated with a high-society party than potluck in a seedy boardinghouse. I sighed happily. It wasn't hard to imagine that nothing like it had ever been heard here before!

I was so proud! They had all pulled together and become a kind of family. Everything would be different from now on, I was sure.

I became dimly aware of another presence in the

room and guessed that it was Doc, treading softly to the window seat to check on me before joining the others in the kitchen. He smelled of soap and a manly after-shave lotion.

Satisfied that his patient was resting comfortably, Doc headed for the swinging door. He had just reached it when Patsy, carrying a plate of food, pushed it open from the other side—and knocked him down.

CHAPTER NINE

DOING THE RIGHT THING

Certain rituals were observed without fail at Mrs. Mumson's, whether she was there or not. One of them was listening, as a group, to the radio in the evening. And since Mrs. Mumson had been away (two months now), we were using the parlor for it, too. On one occasion Teddy had carried the old radio into the parlor from its accustomed place in the dining room, and it had simply stayed. Every night since then we had gathered around it, lounging on the sofa, chairs, or the floor, as we pleased.

We never missed "I Love a Mystery," which we listened to in the dark. *It was so much scarier that way! Just the music alone was enough to give you the heebie-jeebies!* The theme music was Saint-Saens' "Danse Macabre," and very appropriate, too, for a program where the heroes got themselves into the most sinister scrapes, night after night.

When "I Love a Mystery" was over (and if you still had the nerve!) you could tune in to "Gangbusters," which came on right afterward. But if Teddy was there, we skipped it. Teddy objected to "Gangbusters." Didn't like "cop shows," he said. (Was it because he was a gangster?) And in the choice of radio programs, as in most things, Teddy was the boss.

And so, on that fateful September evening, Patsy turned the radio off at 8:30, while the program announcer was saying, "The further adventures of Doc, Jack, and Reggie will come to you tomorrow night at this same hour! 'I Love a Mystery' is brought to you Monday through Friday by—" At the same time, she switched on the tall floor lamp, which chased some of the gloom from the parlor, but I was still jumping at shadows. "Oooooh! Trapped in a temple of vampires! How will they ever get out of *that* one?"

Patsy frowned. "Maybe we shouldn't let Smitty listen to these programs." She was looking to Doc for support. "Might give her nightmares, don't you think?"

Before Doc could offer an opinion, Iris jumped in with, "Talk about nightmares! What'd we have to eat last night?" I said it was lamb patties, and waited for the inevitable complaint. "Yeah, but if that green stuff was mint sauce, it wasn't like any I ever had before!" I explained that it wasn't mint sauce. I didn't have any mint, so I substituted green jalapeno peppers. (Didn't Miss Kitchen encourage creativity and innovation in the wartime cook?) Iris said it was no wonder she had dreamed she was a fire-eater in the circus!

After the radio programs we would share the day's

news, as reported in the evening paper. That night, Teddy had first crack at the front page. "Hey, Howie! Get a load of this! The chairman of a select Senate committee was out here this week to investigate reports of labor being wasted in some West Coast essential industries. Says he found young, able-bodied men clocking in every morning and not doing any work!"

Howard looked up from the Gardening Section and asked languidly why that would interest him. With mock innocence, Teddy replied, "Well, it says here he visited the cannery!"

Teasing Howard on any subject that he was extremely sensitive about (his religion, for one, his job as a supervisor at the cannery, for another) was a sure way to get Howard's goat, as Teddy well knew.

But Howard always bit like a Bigmouth Bass, and all Teddy had to do was reel him in. Jumping up and snatching the paper, he said, "What? Let me see that!" But after scanning the whole article and finding no mention of the cannery, he stalked back to his seat, scowling at Teddy.

I sighed. Things hadn't changed, after all.

"Who was that big shot?" Patsy wanted to know. "That chairman of the what's-it committee?" Teddy said it was some junior senator from Missouri, by the name of Harry Truman. We all went back to reading the paper.

Iris asked Teddy to pass her another section of the paper, and Teddy obliged by handing her the Woman's

Page. "Here you go, Iris. You can read all about the new fall fashions!" Iris told him tersely to give her the Sports Page and to button his lip.

Patsy said she'd like the Entertainment Section. She felt like taking in a movie that weekend. Teddy made a paper airplane out of the movie page and shot it over to Patsy, who unfolded it and began looking over the choices. "Well, there's 'Casablanca.' Seven stars, it says: Humphrey Bogart, Ingrid Bergman, Peter Lorre, Paul Henreid, Sydney Greenstreet, Claude Rains, and Conrad Veidt. Sounds terrif!"

Teddy said he'd seen it, and it wasn't bad. Then he winked at me and said, "Here's lookin' at *you*, kid!"

Patsy asked if I wanted to take in a movie with her, and I said sure. (But I secretly hoped she wouldn't pick "Casablanca," because I had already seen it—with Teddy, as it happened.)

Iris pounded her fist on the arm of her chair, making us all jump. "Hot damn! Babe Didrikson won the Pebble Beach tourney! Now there's a real woman for you!" Teddy allowed the Babe was a great golfer, but who said she was a woman? Iris ground out her cigarette. "I got news for you, Soberjowski! A girl doesn't have to look like Rita Hayworth to be a real woman!"

"Maybe not, but it sure helps! . . . And, anyway, can she run a streetcar?"

"Can *who* run a streetcar?"

"Babe Didrikson! It says right here that not one woman in a thousand can qualify for the job of running a streetcar. 'They have no sense of time,' according to the president of the local transportation company."

"Babe Didrikson has better things to do with *her* time than running a damn streetcar!" Iris lit another cigarette and went back to the Sports Page.

"Better not let the colonel hear you say that!" Teddy had jerked a thumb in the direction of the portrait over the sideboard. I asked if Mr. Mumson was really a colonel.

Patsy giggled. "The only thing we know for sure is that he was off his *trolley*. In more ways than one!"

Doc supplied the details. "It seems the poor man forgot to set the brake before getting out to change the overhead track, and he was run over by his own streetcar."

Teddy liked bizarre or ridiculous news items he found in the paper. He said they balanced the more serious and sometimes ugly war news. "Listen. Here's a lady who's suing her husband for divorce. Seems he took her false teeth away so she couldn't eat meat and he could have all her red stamps!" Patsy accused him of making that one up, but Teddy denied it. "What's more, she's asking for her teeth back in lieu of alimony!"

I was hanging on the back of Teddy's chair and reading over his shoulder (I didn't rate a section of the paper all to myself), when a small headline caught my eye. "I knew it! They're going to ration prunes!"

Oddly enough, I seemed to be the only one discon-

E. E. SMITH

certed by that bit of news. A murmured "Thank God!" was the only response from the others.

Patsy spotted an article she thought would interest Margaret. Where *was* Margaret, she wondered.

It was only then that I realized Margaret hadn't been there for the radio programs. Had she even come down for dinner? I couldn't remember. Poor, mousy little Margaret was so quiet most of the time that it was easy not to notice her absence. Doc said she most likely was still up in her room, lying down. He'd seen her coming out of the bathroom looking pale and asked if she were all right. She had told him she was "just tired" and wanted to lie down for a while.

That was the last that anyone could remember about seeing Margaret.

Patsy put down the movie page. "Listen! Sounds like a car in the driveway."

A car in the driveway was an exciting event. I ran to the window. "It's a taxi. And it looks like Mrs. Mumson in the back."

Then everyone was at the window. "It *is* Mumsy!" said Patsy. Iris volunteered to go out and help the old girl with her gear. Doc said he would go, too, and Patsy said, "Let's all go!"

As everyone except Howard trooped out through the front door, I headed in the other direction, to the kitchen. Mrs. Mumson would want a cup of tea and a snack as soon as she had settled in her usual chair, or I would miss my guess!

Howard had stopped at the bottom of the stairs. He was looking up, and I caught a glimpse of Margaret slowly making her way down. Though they spoke softly, at first, I heard what they had to say while I was filling the big copper tea kettle and setting it on the stove to boil.

And I must confess it was no accident. True, without even trying I could have heard some of their conversation through the swinging door that never quite closed. With a little effort, however, I could hear all of it. And, like their previous talk, it left me shaken.

"Are you all right, Margaret? I was worried."

"Were you, Howard?"

"Of course I was!"

"I'm worried, too."

"You mean about . . . ? Look, Margaret. I've been thinking—"

"You have?"

"I've been thinking that we want to be sure and do the right thing here."

"Oh, Howard! Thank God!" (There was such relief in her voice!)

"No, wait! You don't understand! I mean we want to get out of this . . . in the right way."

"What did you say? Get *out*?"

"Well, yes. Here's what I was thinking, Margaret. There are *ways*, you know, to . . . well, you read about it sometimes. Girls have accidents. They don't get hurt.

Not *themselves*. But it's . . . effective. They might fall down the stairs, or—"

"What? What are you *saying*, Howard?" (Her voice was barely below a scream.)

"Well, what *choice* have we got?" (His voice was rising, too, and there was finally a note of desperation in it.)

"I can think of one." (Her voice was strong and steady now.)

"You can?"

"Yes. It's called 'marriage,' Howard! Our parents did it, and our grandparents did it, and—"

"I can't speak for your parents, but I know that *mine* would never enter into the holy state of matrimony like this! With a *sin* on their heads!"

"Oh, God! I've been living in a fool's paradise. I really thought that, in the end, you would . . ."

I heard Margaret running back up the stairs, and she was sobbing. *I swear, at that moment I never wanted to bean somebody as bad as I wanted to bean that creep Howard!* I peeked out through the swinging door. He was still standing at the bottom of the stairs, staring up into the void at the top.

While I watched, the big front door flew open and Mrs. Mumson and her noisy entourage, loaded down with her luggage and all talking at once, came in— blissfully unaware of the tragic scene that had been played out in the front hall only seconds earlier.

"My goodness!" panted Mrs. Mumson, cooling her hot face with the little fan on a stick, "Let me catch my breath, everybody!" She was nearly on top of Howard before she noticed him standing there, pale and mute. "Oh, hello, Howard. I didn't see you." But Howard didn't answer nor even seem to know she was speaking to him. I guessed it was safe to come out of the kitchen.

Mrs. Mumson was going on about what to do with her things. "Just leave the bags down here for the time being. We can take them upstairs after I've had a chance to rest." Then she surprised everyone by throwing her arms open wide and doing a pirouette right there in the hall, the wooden-handled carpet bag on her wrist nearly sweeping the telephone off its stand. After breathing in the familiar air of the old house, she cried, "My, but it's good to be home!"

Poor Mrs. Mumson! How could she know that her euphoric homecoming was about to be shattered by the time bomb ticking away upstairs?

Finally noticing that she had not been greeted by the stony figure at the bottom of the stairs, Mrs. Mumson asked, "What's the matter, Howard? Cat got your tongue?" But before Howard could respond, she spied me hovering in the dining room. "And here's Eileen, too! Why, I declare, child, I think you've grown while I've been away!"

Teddy said pointedly that I'd had *time* enough to grow a *foot*, and Mrs. Mumson said, "Well, I never dreamed

I'd be gone so long." (We never did, either, Teddy said even more pointedly, but she took no notice.) The lady was making a beeline for her favorite chair in the dining room. The ancient brown leather creaked in protest as her bulky frame was lowered into it.

As predicted, the next words out of her mouth were about food. "I wonder if there's a cup of tea about the place?" This, I knew, was an appeal to me as she busied herself unpinning her green felt hat that looked like a limp artichoke. The rest of her resembled a plump eggplant in the purplish dress and jacket my mother had recently sewn for her. I tried not to smile at the thought: She looked for all the world like a Victory garden.

I shook off the image. "Yes, ma'am," I said, already on my way to the kitchen.

I was pouring boiling water into the good china teapot and setting it carefully on the tray next to a plate of Molasses Oatmeal Cookies (made without sugar) when I heard Mrs. Mumson complaining, "I'm nearly famished from that awful train ride. The dining cars are so inadequate nowadays, what with all the shortages, don't you know."

And then I heard my father's voice growling in my ear: Famished, my foot! Just look at her. "Inadequate dining cars," is it? Why, she ought to take a ride in a *troop train*, now and again! Someone ought to tell her that the railroads are stretched thin providing enough cars, personnel, and provisions to get our boys to and from their ships. Someone ought to remind her that there's a *war* on!

Yes, Daddy. But don't expect me to do it.

I pushed open the swinging door with my shoulder, careful not to tip the tea tray. Iris was asking Mrs. Mumson why she hadn't wired that she was coming. "One of us would have met you at the station—" and Howard added snidely, "That's right, Mumsy. Teddy could've met you in style! He's got a Cadillac now, y'know. Gas is no problem, either. He just got his 'C' card renewed!"

Mrs. Mumson was busy spooning sugar into her tea, so Patsy said, "Better be careful where you park, Teddy. A girl at work got *her* gas card taken away, just for parking near a theater."

"Why?" asked Mrs. Mumson, discreetly dunking a cookie in her teacup. "What's wrong with parking near a theater?"

Patsy explained it was the new ban on pleasure driving. "Get caught near a place of entertainment, and you can kiss your gas card goodbye!"

Teddy grinned. "Don't be a wet blanket, dreamboat! I figured on taking you and Slugger to the movies this weekend." Then he turned to Mrs. Mumson and asked, "What about your Chinese maid, Mumsy?"

Mrs. Mumson seemed to have forgotten all about Yukie. "My what? Oh, you mean . . . ? Well, I wished I could've *kept* Yukie. He was a lifesaver. Always getting me something from that wretched diner before they'd run out of food!"

Teddy said, a trifle impatiently, "But he *did* jump off the train as it slowed down for Tulelake, didn't he?"

"Not in my spectator pumps, I hope," said Patsy. Mrs. Mumson assured her that Yukie was wearing his own clothes by then. But that reminded her: He had sent Patsy's clothes back to her (they were in one of the bags in the hall) and a note, too. Now, where was it?

It took some minutes of rummaging through the faded carpet bag before Mrs. Mumson finally came up with a folded piece of paper. "Yes. Here it is." And she handed the note to Patsy to read while she brushed the cookie crumbs off her broad, eggplant-colored lap.

Patsy read the note aloud. "Dear Miss Patsy," (it began). "I'm sending your clothes back with Mrs. Mumson. Thanks for letting me use them, but I'm sure glad I don't have to wear girl's stuff all the time!"

"It was that girdle," Mrs. Mumson put in. "He complained about it the whole trip."

Patsy said she could *dig* it, and then went on to read the rest of the note: "I know what I'm going to do now. If the war lasts 'til I'm eighteen I'm going to join the 442nd. If they'll take me."

Mrs. Mumson wondered what he meant by that. "The 442nd *what?*"

"The 442nd Army combat team," said Teddy. "An all Japanese-American unit, and a crackerjack outfit!"

"If they'll take him," said Howard gloomily. He was slouching against the sideboard. "If they'll take him," he repeated for emphasis.

> "No loyal citizen of the United States should be denied the democratic right to exercise the responsibilities of his citizenship, regardless of his ancestry. The principle on which this country was founded and by which it has always been governed is that Americanism is a matter of the mind and heart; Americanism is not, and never was, a matter of race or ancestry."
>
> *(President Franklin D. Roosevelt, February 1, 1943 upon activating the 442nd Regimental Combat Team.")*
>
> # "Go For Broke"
> # The motto of the 442nd Regimental Combat Team, All Japanese-American Unit

President Roosevelt's Statement on activating the 442nd Combat Unit.

"They'll take him," said Teddy.

That nettled Howard. That, and Teddy's smirk that spoke again of inside information, his air of confidence that he was right, and *knowing* he was right. It was maddening. "How do you know so much about it?" he snapped.

But Teddy ignored him. "Go on, Patsy."

"I hope I didn't run your stockings," (the note ended), "And it's signed . . . That's funny."

Mrs. Mumson stopped brushing the crumbs off her lap and looked up. "What is, dear?"

"Well, it's signed Woodrow Wilson Matsumoto!"

"Who?"

"Listen. There's a P.S.—That's my real name."

A silence followed in which each of us tried to reconcile a mental image of the boy called Yukie and a newly-minted Woodrow Wilson Matsumoto. Then Mrs. Mumson said, "Strange that we never knew his real name, isn't it? But then, I suppose no one ever asked him." Shaking off any twinge of regret that such a realization may have caused her, she said brightly, "Well, now. What's been going on around here while I was away?"

"Oh, not much," said Teddy matter-of-factly. "You're about to lose half your boarders, is all!"

"I'm *what?*"

Patsy explained. "What he means is, Doc and I both got our orders. I made it into the Navy's interpreter program, and Doc joined the—"

At that moment there was a sharp, piercing cry from upstairs. I froze, along with everyone else. My heart began to wobble like a top spinning out of control.

"Merciful heavens!" cried Mrs. Mumson. "What was *that?*"

Doc was racing for the stairs. "Sounded like Margaret!"

Mrs. Mumson's hands flew up to her face. "My stars! I forgot all about . . . !" Then, turning to Patsy, she said, "Is she . . . is she . . . *you* know?" But Patsy only shrugged helplessly, so Mrs. Mumson wheeled around and confronted Teddy. Wagging an accusing finger at him, she said sharply, "Teddy! It's time we knew what's been going on between you and that unfortunate girl!"

But Teddy wasn't listening to her. Doc was shouting from the head of the stairs, "Somebody call the hospital! Tell them to send an ambulance! Code red!"

Mrs. Mumson shrieked, "Oh, Lord! What is it, Doc?"

"Tell them it's a possible *suicide!*"

Teddy was already at the telephone. "Operator! Operator! This is an emergency!"

The time bomb had gone off.

CHAPTER TEN

GROWING UP

The summer of 1943 had been one of the hottest in anyone's memory, and for Mrs. Mumson and the rest of us in the boardinghouse, one that would not soon, if ever, be forgotten. It had been a summer of change, upheaval, and heartbreak. And for me, at the formative age of eleven, a time to grow up. Perhaps a little too fast.

And it was not over yet.

School would be starting the following week, and I would be leaving the boardinghouse for the last time. A little less then four months, that's how long I had been there. It seemed more like a lifetime to me. I would be leaving behind an experience that few young girls have had (and fewer still would want!) and I would cherish it forever.

In the kitchen on that last Saturday morning, I was preparing breakfast for a dwindling number of boarders, not in my usual striped pinafore uniform but a new dance costume of blue satin bibbed shorts over a white ruffled blouse. My black patent leather tap shoes shone like mirrors (my father would have been proud!) and my hair was tied back with a blue satin ribbon.

Miss Elizabeth had laid down an ultimatum, delivered to my mother during an unusually stormy dress fitting at our house the week before: If I did not show up for this morning's stage show at the Alhambra Theater, I would find there was no place for me in her new fall classes beginning next month! My truancy from dance recitals, and even from lessons, was boiling over into resentment on all sides. Knowing I had better not antagonize Miss Elizabeth or my mother any further, I persuaded a girl in my tap class to come to the boardinghouse after supper one evening and teach me the routine for this Saturday morning's performance. (It would cost me a Storybook Doll out of my collection.) I ran through a few steps now, while gathering up a tray of things for the table.

From the kitchen I heard Mrs. Mumson heavily descending the stairs, making her way to the sideboard and pouring herself a cup of coffee from the pot I had put there only minutes before. Who, I wondered idly, would polish the big silver urn after I'd gone? No one. I pictured the poor thing growing blacker and more unsightly until the day it would finally join the burnt-out toaster and the broken waffle iron on the shelf in the basement.

I was on the verge of pushing open the swinging door with a tray of dishes when I heard Mrs. Mumson give a loud sniff and address Mr. Mumson's portrait above the sideboard.

"Oh, Jack!" she sobbed, and blew her nose loudly. "What a summer this has been!" *Boy, I'll say! I felt about fifty years older by the end of that summer, and if she felt the same way, why, that would make her about a hundred and ten!*

I set the tray down on the sink and listened as Mrs. Mumson continued her conversation (if you could call it that) with Mr. Mumson. I glanced up at the big kitchen clock on the wall. How long should I wait, I wondered. Judging from her emotional state, it might be a while before the "seance" was over.

"You think I should have kept a closer watch on those young people, don't you? You think if I'd paid more attention, I might have prevented everything that happened. But I declare, Jack! You can have people in your own home, day after day, and never really know what's in their hearts!" She paused again to blow her nose. "And what was in poor Margaret's heart? Did she really mean to kill herself? I still don't know."

She paused again, longer this time, and I felt I had waited a respectful interval before barging in, so I picked up my tray. But not quickly enough. The rattling of last night's newspaper, which I had folded and left by the side of the old brown leather armchair, accompanied a fresh outburst. "Oh, there's too *much* killing nowadays! And everything else, too, what with so many boys coming home from the war, wounded in body and spirit. In this kind of a world, is it any wonder that decent family life has become a thing of the past?" Then she added fiercely (and prophetically), "We'll never be the same in this country, Jack!"

I pushed open the swinging door, in a hurry this time, before she could begin again. But she was only staring sadly at the pictures in the newspaper of the wounded—some able to walk, some being carried on stretchers—returning from the war zones.

She looked up and managed a smile when I said good morning to her. "Well, now, don't you look cute? What kind of a dance are you doing today?"

I said it was a tap routine, although that much should have been obvious from the clickety-clack my shoes were making on the bare wood floor.

"See, I'm supposed to be a farmer*ette*, and the stage is a Victory garden. Trouble is, I have to dance with a hoe and I'm scared I'll trip over it!" (I had practiced with a real hoe in the back yard and knew I had good reason to be worried.)

Mrs. Mumson tried to sound reassuring. "I'm sure you won't do that, dear." *She hadn't seen me almost break my fool neck in the back yard!* I asked if she would mind if I stayed for the Lone Ranger movie right after the stage show. She said that would be fine. "You run along and enjoy yourself," and after another glance at the war pictures in the paper, she added, "while you can."

The war, a rash of unsettling events in her own home, and perhaps feeling her age a bit (she was a grandmother now, after all) had caused my employer to mellow in a way I would not have thought possible at first.

I paused in setting the table. "How many will be here this morning?"

Mrs. Mumson sighed. "I never know anymore. But you'd better set a place for Margaret, too. What time did Teddy say she was getting out?"

Before I could say that Teddy had left for the hospital about an hour ago, I heard his car pulling into the driveway. Not in his usual brash manner, with brakes squealing and music blaring from the radio. No, today his approach was decidedly subdued. Teddy was carrying a fragile passenger.

"That might be them, now."

But Mrs. Mumson had heard it, too. Suddenly galvanized into action, she heaved herself out of her chair and scurried off to the parlor to busy herself doing unnecessary things. She was fluffing the pillows on the sofa when she whispered in an absurdly conspiratorial tone, "All right now, dear!" and giving the last one a thump that made the dust fly, she said, "We must do our best to be kind, don't you know, and show Margaret that we're glad she's home!" While polishing a fingerprint off a metal lamp with her apron, she said, "You read so many awful things about people who . . . why, they say most of them try it again if they fail the first time!" And, although I had said nothing at all, she added, "Shhhh! Here they are, now."

Like two mute statues, we listened for footsteps in the hall.

And then she was there, framed by the french doors, a pale and pathetic little Margaret in a shapeless cotton sweater and skirt. Her dull brown hair, usually wound into a bun at the back of her neck, was hanging loose about her thin shoulders. Not quite hidden under her sleeves were gauze bandages on both wrists that covered the gashes made with a broken water glass in the bathroom three weeks earlier. That was the night Margaret stopped living in what she had called her "fool's paradise," and might have stopped living altogether if there had not been a doctor in the house.

Teddy was close behind. He set her small tan suitcase down in the hall and, putting a firm hand under her elbow, led a shaky Margaret down the three familiar steps and into the sunny parlor.

Mrs. Mumson rushed forward, arms outstretched. "Margaret! I'm so glad to see you! Welcome home, dear!"

For one awful moment I thought the good lady was going to take hold of Margaret's wrists, bandages and all! But she spied them just in time to stop herself in mid-flight. "Oh, my dear!" she exclaimed, wide-eyed. All the color drained from her face and I even wondered if she might faint, but she recovered in seconds and cooed, "Come and sit down. How pale you look! And thin! Didn't they feed you at that old hospital?"

Clasping Margaret around her bony shoulders, Mrs.

Mumson propelled her toward the dining room, saying, "Let's get you something to eat!" And although she seemed willing, even eager, to show the utmost kindness to Margaret, she soon made it clear that her largesse did not extend to Teddy. Scowling at him over her shoulder, she said, "I suppose *you'll* want something, too!"

The British have an expression: getting hold of the wrong end of the stick. Mrs. Mumson had certainly got hold of the wrong end of the stick about who was to blame for Margaret's "being in a family way." Teddy didn't care "two pins" for rules, she had said often enough. Teddy was mysterious and evasive, even about what he did for a living, which left him open to suspicions of every kind.

Of course, I had never told anyone about the conversations I had overheard between Margaret and Howard.

If Teddy noticed Mrs. Mumson's less than gracious invitation to breakfast, he didn't show it. "Thanks," he said with a wink at me as he headed out again through the french doors, "I've got things to do upstairs."

Mrs. Mumson's mind quickly returned to breakfast. "Let's see. What can we give her, Eileen?"

As it happened, I had made Cheese Blintzes for breakfast, and a large platter of them was being kept warm in the oven at that very moment. It was my German grandmother's recipe, not anything I had seen in Miss Kitchen's column. *To be honest, I was beginning to think Miss Kitchen might be a phony, that maybe there never was a Miss Kitchen—or worse, that "she" was a "he!"*

Mrs. Mumson guided Margaret to her old chair at the table, but once there, Margaret said she really didn't want anything to eat.

Well, we would see about *that!* I slipped past them into the kitchen and dished up two golden brown blintzes onto a small plate, topping each with a spoonful of my own strawberry jam.

Back in the dining room Mrs. Mumson was pouring coffee along with a steady stream of advice. Margaret must *eat* if she expected to get well and strong again. "We want to see the roses back in your cheeks!" she declared. (Try as I may, I could not picture a strong and rosy-cheeked Margaret!)

After that there was silence (the eye of the storm, I figured. Sure enough, anguished words followed): "Mumsy, you don't know how sorry I am for what I've done—to *all* of us!"

Mrs. Mumson hesitated only slightly before she said, "It's all right, Margaret." But I knew it wasn't.

Margaret knew it, too. "No! Three weeks in a psychiatric ward have given me a lot of time to think!"

Mrs. Mumson was doing her best to be sympathetic, but it was a struggle. She had too much on her mind, questions without any satisfactory answers; the whole business needed clearing up. But it would have to wait.

"What you need to be thinking about now is getting well and putting all this behind you!" she said stoutly. And she was obviously relieved to announce, "Now, here's Eileen with your breakfast," as I pushed open the swinging door.

Even Mrs. Mumson didn't know what Cheese Blintzes were, but she did recognize my strawberry jam. "Eileen made it herself," she said proudly. And I quickly assured Margaret that there were no beets in it (a reference to the much-maligned Fourth of July beet ice cream).

Margaret managed a faint smile and then said something I found hard to believe. She said she had missed my cooking! "The hospital food was so . . . *ordinary*, by comparison."

Mrs. Mumson told Margaret that this was my last week. "She has to go back to school on Monday, and I declare I don't know what I'll do without her!"

She had not found anyone to replace me and I knew she wouldn't, at least not until the war was over. For that reason, although I hadn't told her or even asked my mother yet, I was planning to come back on occasional weekends to help out.

Was that the reason? To help out? Or was it to see Teddy?

Margaret said the place wouldn't be the same without "our Smitty." And I had to confess that going back to school was going to seem pretty dull after this summer!

Mrs. Mumson quickly changed the subject. "Patsy

and Doc are gone, too, Margaret. There's only Iris and Howard now." She frowned. "And Teddy, of course." With that, Mrs. Mumson's forbearance came to an abrupt end. "Margaret, I do want to have a word with you about Teddy. In light of what's happened, I'm afraid I must insist—" but her lecture was interrupted by the unexpected ringing of the doorbell. "Now, who can that be?" she said with some annoyance.

I said, "I'll get it!" and bolted into the hall with a terrific clatter, forgetting that I was wearing tap shoes.

I opened the heavy front door to an American beauty rose in navy blue. For there, in her smart WAVE uniform and pert little hat, stood our very own Patsy.

"What's buzzin', cousin?"

For an instant I was too surprised to say anything. Then I squeaked, "Wow! What a swell uniform!"

From the dining room an equally astonished Mrs. Mumson exclaimed, "Why, it's Patsy!" and called out, "Patsy! In here, dear!"

We went in together, but I was careful to stay on the carpet runner so as to dampen the noise my shoes were making on our march to the dining room.

"What a lovely surprise!" crowed Mrs. Mumson when she saw Patsy. "And how wonderful you look!"

Patsy gave Mrs. Mumson a hug before turning to greet Margaret, whom I guessed she hadn't recognized at first. Then, as it dawned on her that the bedraggled creature slumped at the table was her old roommate, she cried out, "Margaret! Gosh, it's good to see you!"

Margaret said it was good to see her, too. And I knew she meant it, though she must have been painfully aware of the stark contrast between herself and Patsy, who was even more attractive as a WAVE than a pin-up girl. Gone was the vibrant red lipstick and matching nail polish, but there was a new and very becoming radiance under the softer makeup. The high-heeled sandals had been packed away, and her Betty Grable legs now ended in sensible black pumps. A navy blue skirt and jacket had replaced the little Angora sweaters and white shorts, but still showed off her perfect figure. I was thinking that Patsy seemed almost embarrassed to look the way she did, when there was poor Margaret . . .

But Mrs. Mumson jumped into the breech with typical southern charm. "Oh, I do hope you can stay a while," she purred.

Patsy took off her hat and ran her fingers through the soft yellow curls of her new, shorter hairdo. "I wish I could, Mumsy, but I've only got a few minutes."

She had a cab waiting, she said. In fact, she had only come to look for one of her Japanese language books, which she thought might still be up in her old room.

"I meant to pack it, natch, but with so much going on . . . I mean—" It was an unintentional slip of the tongue, that reference to grim events that had turned the household upside down three weeks ago.

Again Mrs. Mumson rescued the moment. "Why, I

haven't seen your book, Patsy. But you're welcome to look around upstairs." Then, dismissing all thoughts of a cab in the driveway with its meter running, she said, "Why don't you sit down and have some coffee first. Have you had breakfast? Eileen has made some simply beautiful, uh, what did you call them, dear?"

I didn't get a chance to tell her about the blintzes. Patsy was already saying, again, that she wished she had more time, but she had to catch a 10:30 train to Washington, D.C. But why not come upstairs with her? "We can talk while I look for that book. You, too, Smitty!"

"No can do, Patsy. The show must go on, y'know!" I did a quick Shuffle off to Buffalo and a stage bow to illustrate the point.

Mrs. Mumson remarked on how I had changed since she first took me on, four months ago. "Why, I feel as though I've watched this girl grow up," she said with a tinge of sadness. "Just over the summer, don't you know."

It was true that I had grown. The little pink and white uniform my mother had made only last June was beginning to feel tight across the chest, and the white shoes were a half size too small for me now.

I gathered up Margaret's breakfast dishes, noting with satisfaction that she had eaten one whole Cheese Blintz, strawberry jam and all. She and Mrs. Mumson went upstairs with Patsy and I took the dishes into the kitchen.

The water in the sink may have been running when the doorbell rang again, because I never heard it. What I did hear a minute later was a "Yoo hoo! . . . Is anybody home?" It was a man's voice. Someone had let himself into the front hall. That was odd, but my hands were in a pan of soapy water and anyway I thought I heard Mrs. Mumson coming down the stairs to see who it was.

But it wasn't Mrs. Mumson. It was Patsy and she was calling, "Hey, Smitty! Did you find some class notes in my room?"

I dried my hands quickly. The notes were in a box in the hall closet. I pushed open the kitchen door but stopped dead in my tracks when I caught sight of our latest visitor. A tall man in a Navy uniform might have been anyone. But the hair, looking for all the world like a nest of twisted red twigs, was unmistakable.

Doc and Patsy, in their new roles as WAVE and Navy doctor, were coming face to face at the bottom of the stairs.

Patsy dropped the book she was carrying. "Doc! I didn't know *you* were here!" and Doc stammered, "I didn't know I was here, either! . . . I mean . . . I mean I didn't know *you* were here, either!"

From behind the half-open kitchen door I could see that under the fine-tailored uniform with its double row of gold buttons, Doc's heart still beat for Patsy— and just the sight of her could still short-circuit his brain!

Doc bent down to retrieve the book at Patsy's feet. "Here, let me get it. Better watch your head. Remember?"

With the book safely back in her hands, and after an awkward silence, Patsy said, "I'm so glad to see you, Doc! When did you get here?"

"A couple of minutes ago. I just dropped in to say goodbye one last time."

"But I thought you left right after I did, three weeks ago."

"Well, yes, I did. But now I've got new orders and I'm leaving the state. I've been assigned to a hospital on the East Coast." Then, pointing out the window, he said, "So that's your cab out there, is it?"

"That's right. I just came by for this book. I've got new orders, too. I'm leaving this morning."

Doc said he was certainly glad he got to see her once more, and even ventured a shy, "You look terrific!"

"So do you, Doc! That uniform *does* something for you!"

Doc looked down at his shiny black shoes and said, "Thanks. Oh, and how do you like the interpreter program?"

Patsy said it was fine so far, and explained the reason she was going to Washington. There was a school there.

Doc stopped studying his shoes. "You're going to Washington? You mean Washington, D.C.?"

As though explaining geography to a third-grader, Patsy said, "That's where the school is, yes."

"But that's great! I've been assigned to the new Naval hospital at Bethesda. Just outside Washington!"

"Practically spitting distance!"

I watched Doc rolling his hat in his hands. "Do you think I could see you sometime? . . . If I came into Washington?"

"Of course, Doc. That'd be great!"

What followed was one of those moments you only see in old movies, where the shy hero sways forward, tantalizingly close to the object of his desire, only to lose his nerve at the last second.

Patsy waited for the kiss that never came. After a moment she said, "Well, my cab's waiting."

"So is mine."

"You mean there are *two* cabs out there with their meters running?"

"Looks like it."

"Well . . . do we really *need* two cabs?"

I couldn't hear Doc's answer, and I couldn't see what happened next, but when I heard the front door close, I crept out of my hiding place and ran to the window.

Mrs. Mumson was just coming down the stairs. "Why, where's Patsy? Did she leave?"

"Two taxis are pulling out of the driveway. One's empty, and Patsy and *Doc* are in the *other* one!"

"Doc, did you say? Was he here? I declare, I can't keep up with anything anymore!"

"He's kissing her, too!"

"Now, Eileen, you see entirely too much for a girl your age!" she scolded. But she was smiling, too.

Margaret came down the stairs, saying, "I just saw Patsy leaving with someone. And I could swear it was Doc!"

Mrs. Mumson said excitedly, "It *was* Doc! And what do you think? It looks like they finally got together!"

E. E. SMITH

CHAPTER ELEVEN

SAYING GOODBYE

The happy ending to the story of Doc and Patsy, Mrs. Mumson would soon discover, was only a small island in her sea of troubles.

She and Margaret had returned to the table for another cup of coffee and a little gossip about the future of the WAVE and Navy doctor. (Mrs. Mumson said she envisioned a tasteful wedding with crossed swords in a Navy chapel or perhaps a garden in Washington, D.C.)

Teddy came back into the dining room, herding Howard in front of him like a schoolboy being sent to the principal's office.

"So, what is it you want to show me, Soberjowski? If this is another one of your jokes—" but he stopped dead when he saw who was sitting at the table with Mrs. Mumson. "Margaret! What are you doing here?"

Margaret said coolly, "They let me out this morning. Didn't you know?"

Howard stammered, "No. I . . . How did you . . . ?"

"Teddy brought me home." There was a slight toss

of her head. "He came to see me every day in the hospital, too!"

"What? They told me you couldn't have visitors!"

"Well, Teddy managed it all right!"

That was too much. Howard's old resentment toward Teddy boiled over into real anger this time. "Okay, Houdini! Tell us how you did that."

In mock innocence, Teddy replied, "Oh, you know me! More pull than a souped-up vacuum cleaner!"

"Yeah. Seems like there's nothing our Teddy can't do!"

Teddy's voice was calm, but there was a sharp edge to it. "Listen, Junior. You're a big boy now. Why don't you grow up?"

I had learned at an early age to know when trouble was brewing, and it was brewing now. Time for me to beat a hasty retreat to the sanctity of my kitchen!

Mrs. Mumson seemed relieved when I had left the room. She always felt easier about discussing delicate subjects without "little pitchers with big ears" in attendance. *She never did figure out that I could see and hear most everything through that door that wouldn't close!*

"Now that you're here, Teddy," Mrs. Mumson began, "I want to have a talk with you and Margaret." She tried to dismiss Howard by saying, "Howard, this doesn't concern you." But Margaret said, "I wouldn't be too sure, Mumsy."

"Oh? Well, you've all been warned that I have very strict rules of conduct in my house. That means no fraternizing between my boys and girls." So far she was on fairly safe ground. "And when a girl gets herself in trouble—" Now she wasn't so sure. "Dear me! What a silly expression that is! I mean, of course, when a girl and *boy* get into trouble—"

Margaret interrupted the lecture with, "I couldn't agree more, Mumsy. It took two of us to get into this mess! But, as usual, it's the girl who is condemned for the sins of both!" She turned and confronted Howard directly. "Isn't that right, Howard? Haven't I been condemned for *our* sins?"

Mrs. Mumson was left totally adrift at that point. She said lamely, "Howard? But I thought . . ."

Howard tried desperately to save his own cowardly skin. "What are you saying, Margaret? That I'm to blame for those?" He was pointing to the gauze bandages on her wrists. "Why are you dragging me into this?" Turning back to Mrs. Mumson, he pleaded, "Believe me, Mumsy, I had nothing to do with it!"

My father used to say that if a man is lying, and you know the truth of the matter, you've got to stand up and say so. If you don't, you're just as much a liar as he is. Or words to that effect.

And that's when I pushed open the swinging door and walked straight into the hornets' nest.

"But you told her she ought to do something, like throwing herself down the stairs. I heard you! The day Mrs. Mumson came home, when everyone went outside except me!" I took a deep breath. My heart was doing a Gene Krupa solo, but there was no turning back now. "And right after that, Margaret cut her wrists!"

A moment of stunned silence greeted the end of my brave little speech. Then, with everyone watching, Howard suddenly lunged at me. I screamed when he grabbed my arm.

"You little brat! I'll teach you to spy on people!"

It all happened so fast that I had no time to think, but I knew that Teddy had broken Howard's grip on me with a vicious karate chop to the wrist. And now Howard was the one howling in pain. In one more lightning-fast move, Teddy spun him around and had his neck in a powerful choke hold. Howard stopped howling—and even breathing!—after that.

Teddy's voice thundered, "You lay your dirty paws on her again and you're gonna be the *next* casualty in this house! Do you read me? . . . Loud and clear?"

Howard was making choking sounds, but Teddy still held him in his vise-like grip. "Just nod your heard, Bird Brain, and lemme hear the rocks rattle!" You could tell that Howard was *trying* to nod his head, and Teddy said, "Right! So we understand each other now?" But he still hung on.

Mrs. Mumson, who had been too horrified to act, finally found her voice. "Teddy! For pity sake! You'll kill him!"

Margaret, too, began to fear for Howard's life. She was pulling at Teddy's sleeve and begging. "Please, Teddy! . . . Don't!"

E. E. SMITH

Howard's face had gone all white by the time Teddy finally released his grip. Gasping for breath and holding his throat, he fell into the big leather armchair.

Teddy stood over him with clenched fists, daring him to get up again.

Mrs. Mumson's horror turned to outrage. "What in the world are we coming to? This used to be a . . . a respectable house! Oh, what would Mr. Mumson say?" It seemed an odd time to worry about a dead man's opinion, but that was her way of coping with whatever went beyond her own ability to comprehend. It was easier simply to defer to Mr. Mumson.

Teddy stood aside when Margaret knelt down beside Howard in the big armchair. She was crying and mopping his face with her own handkerchief. "Are you all right, Howard?" Howard was coughing in between ragged gasps.

Teddy turned to Mrs. Mumson and made a stab at apologizing. "Sorry, Mumsy. I know how you hate—" but Mrs. Mumson finished it for him. "Violence! Common street brawling in my house! I never thought I'd see the day! . . . Oh, where will it all end?"

"Well, if it's any comfort to you, I'll be out of your hair sooner than you think. I'll give you a week's rent in lieu of notice. I was leaving this morning anyway."

Teddy leaving? Until that moment I had been huddled in the corner, holding my injured arm. Now it seemed that another calamity, worse than being beaten up by a bully, was about to befall me!

Teddy came over to me and said, "Let's see your arm, honey." I showed him, in between little sobs. (Was it the pain in my arm or the one in my heart that was making me cry?) "You're gonna have a nasty bruise in a few hours. But there's nothing broken." And to Howard he said sternly, "No thanks to *you*, Bird Brain! And don't ever try that again, see? Not if you know what's good for you. I just might kill you next time!" He was standing over Howard's chair again. "You got that?" Howard quickly nodded his head.

Teddy's continued presence in the dining room was clearly upsetting Mrs. Mumson, so he turned and strode out through the french doors, narrowly avoiding a collision with Iris on her way in. "What the hell's going on?" Iris demanded to know. "What was all that commotion? And where was Teddy going in such a hurry?"

Mrs. Mumson's shaky composure suddenly gave way completely, and she ran to Iris in a flood of tears. Patting the heaving shoulders, Iris said, "There, there, old girl. What's the trouble?"

You could see right away that Mrs. Mumson regretted such a show of weakness in her own dining room. She pulled away abruptly with only a clipped, "I'll tell you about it later." Wiping her red-rimmed eyes, she returned to where I was still cowering in the corner. "Are you hurt, dear? Let me see your arm." I assured her that it was all right. "All that same, we'd better put some ice on it. Come into the kitchen."

With my mind still on the bombshell that Teddy had dropped—he was going away!—I let myself be led through the swinging door while Mrs. Mumson worried aloud about what my mother was going to say about *this!* Iris followed after us pleading, "Will someone please tell me what's going on?"

In the kitchen Mrs. Mumson told Iris to chip half a block of ice into a dishpan, saying she was still too shaken to be trusted not to stab herself! Then they left me at the sink with my arm in ice water up to the elbow, while the two of them huddled in the breakfast nook, drinking tea and talking in hushed tones.

But I wasn't listening. Not to them, anyway. Perched on a high stool at the sink, I was observing the latest scene between Margaret and Howard, now alone in the dining room. I could only see Margaret through the gap in the door, but her remarks were directed to the armchair on the other side of the room.

"How could you say what you did, Howard?—that you had nothing to do with it? You had a great *deal* to do with it!" (I couldn't hear what Howard said, if he said anything at all.) "Well, it doesn't matter. I'm the one who has to live with what I've done, not you." She was twisting her handkerchief in her small hands and biting her lip. "I was raised a Catholic, did you know that? My family would never understand, or forgive me—even if I had the courage to tell them. But just to set the record straight, I wasn't trying to do what you wanted me to." She held up her bandaged wrists. "I did this with no thought of anything except taking my own life . . . Isn't that pathetic? I couldn't even do *that* right!"

Mrs. Mumson swooped by me at that point, pushing her way through the swinging door with such force that it stuck in the wide open position. Clearly, the lady was on a mission.

"Howard," she said to the crumpled figure in the big chair, "I think you will agree, you being a religious person in your own peculiar way, that a man must answer for his sins and be punished for them, as surely as there is a heaven and . . . that other place. Now, I'm not saying that I see the hand of Providence in any of this. However . . ." and here she paused long enough to pull an official-looking envelope out of the top drawer of the sideboard. "However," she began again, with obvious satisfaction, "they do say the Lord moves in mysterious ways!"

Howard's voice was more like a frog croaking. "What've . . . what have you got there?"

"It came for you this morning by special post. You weren't here, so I took the liberty of opening it. Something from the government might be urgent, don't you know."

Howard had struggled to his feet and was reaching for the envelope. "The government? . . . Lemme see!"

But Mrs. Mumson seemed to be enjoying her little game of cat and mouse. She was holding the envelope just out of Howard's reach. "It's from your draft board.

You've been reclassified, if that's what you call it. '1-A,' I think. Or 'A-1.' Something like that, anyway."

Howard risked losing his balance to snatch the envelope from Mrs. Mumson's hand. He yanked out the letter inside and mumbled, "Reclassified . . . 1-A! . . . But I've got an essential job! . . . What about *that?*"

Margaret said she had read recently about certain job categories being declassified because they needed more men. "Does that mean you'll be drafted now?"

Howard's answer was swift, but in the end, futile. "No! Not if . . . Margaret! We'll get married. I'll tell them I'm going to be a father!"

"You *were* going to be a father, Howard," Margaret corrected him.

Howard turned and made for the front hall in a kind of lurching gait. He was waving the letter and croaking, "Drafted! They . . . they can't do this to me!"

It was my final glimpse of the man who vowed only last Fourth of July that he would "join up in a minute" if his job at the cannery were not essential!

A moment later we heard the front door slam. The next streetcar would no doubt take him directly to the Selective Service office downtown. But this was Saturday and he would find it closed.

When he was gone, Margaret said softly, "Poor Howard. I actually feel sorry for him." But Mrs. Mumson would have none of it. "Nonsense, dear. I know what Mr. Mumson would say!" and without so much as a nod to the portrait staring down at her, she declared, "He'd say that Howard brought it all on himself. And personally, I agree."

Margaret's shoulders began to sag. Mrs. Mumson patted her hand and said, "You look exhausted, Margaret. Why don't you go upstairs and rest a while? My word! Another day like this one, and they'll be putting you back in the hospital! And me along with you!"

I dried my arm, which was numb with cold, but the swelling had gone down and I figured the bruise could be hidden with enough stage makeup. I would still be able to dance this morning. The show must go on, I grimly reminded myself.

Iris walked out of the kitchen with me. "So old Teddy really rang Howard's bell, did he? Damn! I wish I'd seen that!"

Mrs. Mumson, returning from seeing Margaret safely up the stairs, scowled disapprovingly.

I looked past Mrs. Mumson and caught a glimpse of Teddy in the hall, putting two suitcases down near the front door. He was wearing a dark gray business suit with a white shirt and a conservative striped tie. *Well, you would never take him for a gangster today!* But where was the gun, I wondered. In the shoulder holster under the suit coat? Or in one of the bags, maybe in its own secret compartment?

Now Teddy was in the parlor, talking to Mrs. Mumson. He was giving her two weeks' rent instead of one, he said. She would need a little extra, with so many of them leaving. Mrs. Mumson hesitated only a split second before snatching the bills Teddy held out to her and tucking them into her ample bosom. I heard her say, "Well, if you insist!" Then, beckoning to Iris in the dining room, she said, "Come upstairs with me, will you, Iris? I just sent Margaret up there and I want to be sure there aren't any sharp objects lying around!"

"Hang on a minute, Mums." Iris was fishing in the pockets of her baggy khaki pants. Counting out some coins, she dropped them on the table. "Here, Smitty. Get me a pack of cigarettes next time you go shopping. The usual, Luckys. Wait, here's thirty cents. Get me two packs."

Teddy and I were alone in the parlor.

"Oh, Teddy! Are you really going to leave?" I was trying not to sound as hysterical as I felt.

"Yeah."

"But why?" Now I was trying not to whine.

"Well, because I was sent here to do a job. Now it's done, and I have to go on to another job. That's how they do things at the . . . at the place where I work."

"Where do you work, Teddy?" I was playing for time now. Anything to keep him from walking out that door! "Howard doesn't believe you're in the used car business. He thinks it's something illegal, and so does Iris!"

"Listen. Don't believe anything Howard tells you. And don't let 'Bull-Dozier' push you around, either!" I didn't understand, so he pointed to the coins on the table. "You give that money back and tell her you're not supposed to buy smokes. You're a *kid!*"

That hurt, so I went into one of my sulks. "Well, you don't have to rub it in!"

"Hey! You'll trip over that lower lip, if you're not careful!" There was that famous grin again. "I'm gonna miss you, Slugger!"

"Oh, Teddy! I'll miss you, too! I wish you wouldn't go!" There was desperation in my voice now, and I could hear my father advising caution: Easy, now! Haven't I always said you have to know when to *fold 'em*, as well as hold 'em? But I threw caution to the wind. "Teddy! Could you wait for me?"

Teddy was still grinning. "What?"

"I'm nearly thirteen." (I had told that lie so often I was beginning to believe it myself!) "Could you wait 'til I'm twenty-one? I could even get married when I'm eighteen, with my mother's permission!"

Teddy wasn't grinning now. He was laughing! "What? *Get married!*"

I was crushed. "But, when you said you'd kill Howard if he ever hurt me again, I started thinking it was 'cause you loved me!"

"Well, I do, honey. But not—"

In for a penny, in for a pound. "And I'll never love anybody but *you*, Teddy!"

Teddy took both my hands in his big strong ones and said gently, "Oh, yes, you will. And you'll forget all about me, too. You'll see! . . . A pretty girl like you?

Why, you'll break a hundred hearts before some lucky guy wins *your* heart!"

That wasn't what I wanted to hear, but I could see that my time for argument was running out. "But why do you have to go? Where are you going?"

"I'm leaving town. That's all I can tell you."

"Are you in trouble?" *Was the mob after him? Or the cops?* Naturally, I had never let on that I knew he carried a gun. But maybe he wasn't a gangster. Maybe he was something else. I tried to remember all those bad things Patsy and Iris had been talking about on my first morning there. "You're not a spy, or a . . . a fifth columnist, are you?"

"No." Then, with a quick look into the hall, to make sure no one else was hearing this, he said, "But I do work for the government."

"Whose government?" (I prayed he meant ours!)

"The United States Government," he assured me with a chuckle. "Now, I gotta get going."

"But, Teddy! Wait! Will I ever see you again? Will you write to me?"

"Sure, I will."

"But what if they put me and my mother into a relocation camp for Germans? How will you know where to write?"

"Don't worry about that. But . . ." He reached into his wallet and took out a business card. "If you ever need me, or have to get in touch with me for any reason, just tell the long distance operator you want this number." Taking a pen out of his shirt pocket, he wrote something on the back of the card. "And when they answer, give them this name. It's a code name. They'll do the rest."

I took the card Teddy handed me, but my eyes never left his face. I was trying to memorize every detail, because I knew I would never see him again.

Putting away the wallet and pen, he started up the steps to the hallway. How many times had I seen him walk up those steps? And now I was seeing it for the very last time!

"But, can't you tell me where you're going?"

He paused on the first step. "No, I can't. And what I told you about working for the government has got to be our little secret, all right?" On the second step, "You want to know something funny? I don't care what the rest of them think of me, so why should it be any different with you?" Then he answered his own question. "It just is, that's all." On the last step he pointed to the card in my hand. "Now, you keep that in a safe place. And don't show it to anyone. Promise?"

I nodded and gripped the card tightly in my sweaty hand.

He was in the hall now, about to pick up his bags, with me dogging his heels. (I still didn't know when to fold 'em!)

"Teddy! Couldn't you come to the Alhambra Theater with me this morning? I'm gonna dance."

"I wish I could. But my train leaves in an hour . . . Goodbye, Slugger."

Then his strong, warm arms wrapped around me one last time (and I knew that the shoulder holster and the gun were in his suitcase). As the front door closed behind him, I sobbed, "Oh, Teddy! What'll I do without you?"

I stood there, stupidly staring at the door and berating myself for making such a mess of things. I had begged and whined. Kids whined, grownup girls didn't! And now here I was, blubbering like a baby. *Why, I hadn't grown up at all!* Teddy had been right. ("You're a *kid!*") And the worst part was risking everything on one last roll of the dice ("Teddy, could you wait for me?") and losing. My father would have been ashamed.

I heard the engine of Teddy's latest hot car (an Oldsmobile sedan he called "Black Beauty") springing to life with a mighty roar. Only then did my thoughts return to the card in my hand. I looked at it for the first time. Through eyes that were swimming with tears, I managed to read what it said:

Federal Bureau of Investigation, Washington, D.C., the telephone number, and then his name, Theodore J. Soberjowski.

I turned the card over and saw the code name he had written there:

"Lone Ranger."

I ran for the window in the parlor, nearly knocking the telephone off its stand in my wild dash down the hallway. "Black Beauty" was making its noisy getaway in the street below. But I was not hearing that. Instead,

I was hearing the distant thunder of hooves and a familiar crescendo from the "William Tell Overture."

And I swear to God I also heard a "Hi Ho Silver! Away!"

CHAPTER TWELVE

STRIKING THE SET

Following the last performance in the run of a stage play there is a ritual called "striking" (or taking apart) the set. A "strike" will be called for a certain hour on a specific day. Then a work crew will assemble on the stage, ready to take up a variety of tools and begin demolishing what had been painstakingly constructed only weeks or months before.

The crew that builds the set may consist of paid professionals in Equity houses, but in smaller and regional theaters it is usually a bunch of amateurs, most of them volunteers, under the direction of someone who (hopefully) knows what he or she is doing, and coordinates the work with the director and the set designer.

The crew that strikes the set may, in fact, be the same ones who built it in the first place and now have the unenviable task of tearing it apart. Occasionally, I still volunteer to help both with building and striking sets (just because I like to hang around a theater). But to me, compared with the fun and excitement of

Endearing cast fills 'Boardinghouse'

By Maureen Conlan
Post Staff Reporter

THEATER REVIEW

Don't miss the poignant and funny "Boardinghouse Stew," about wartime America, which opened Friday at Northern Kentucky University, one of three new plays to receive a world premiere at NKU's YES (Year-End-Series) Festival.

Playwright E. E. Smith has drawn on her own girlhood recollections of working in a boardinghouse during the summer of 1943 to re-create an era. She fleshes it out with a cast of endearing characters.

Eileen, the narrator, is a bright and energetic "going on thirteen" year-old, who comes to help boardinghouse owner, Mrs. Mumson. She is soon running things almost single-handedly, with enthusiasm and a penchant for cooking with prunes and peanuts to save on rations.

BOARDINGHOUSE STEW, at YES Festival, Northern Kentucky University. Director: Joe Conger. Playwright: E. E. Smith. Set Design: Dale Lamson. Play dates: in repertory with "Seed of Darkness" and "The Beast" through April 23. Reservations: 572-5464.

Ellen Schreiber, as Eileen, gives a charming portrayal of a spunky girl on the brink of growing up. She has all the fidgety gestures of an almost-teenager down to a T, and she's got a wonderfully comedic, expressive face.

Mrs. Mumson, who talks to a portrait of her dead husband, mothers her boarders, whom she prefers to call "guests." Mary Jo Beresford is excellent in the role.

The six boarders include Patsy, a pin-up pretty young

woman who uses all the latest lingo. She wants to join the WAVES, and to attract the attention of another one of Mrs. Mumson's boarders, Doc.

As the clumsy Doc, Scott McGee has some funny pratfalls, and he and Patsy, played just right by Nora Gdaniec, have a gem of a collision and dual fall.

As much as being about the war, the play is about these characters and the other boarders, how they care about each other and become a kind of family.

The cast is superb. There is a fine attention to stage gestures and detail of set and props, from radio broadcasts by Walter Winchell to Eileen's much-maligned meals, served on stage.

From the *Cincinnati Post*, April 15, 1989.

building the set, striking it is rather a depressing experience. Sort of like taking down the Christmas tree.

As a playwright—and this may be a good time to confess that *Boardinghouse Stew* was first written and produced as a play—I have a ritual, perhaps uniquely my own, that I follow whenever possible.

I like to visit the set of each of my plays on the last night of the run. Then I can stroll leisurely through the set, taking it all in one more time, after the actors have

E. E. SMITH

adjourned to the Green Room to mingle with the audience and before the strike crew shows up.

The best set I can remember for *Boardinghouse* was the first. The play had been a winner that year in a New Play Competition at the University of Northern Kentucky, and a stipend was provided for travel to the campus for the purpose of seeing the production by their excellent drama department.

The first thing I wanted to do when I arrived on campus was to visit the set, which was still under construction. I walked into the theater and my mouth literally dropped open. They were building an entire house on the stage—one I felt I could move into when it was finished! A gaggle of students on loan from the art department was lovingly painting the "faded roses" on the wallpaper in the parlor. There was even a stove in the kitchen that would cook a real roast beef for the Fourth of July dinner scene—not once, but every night of the run!

The worst (or least successful) set for this same play, in my opinion, was a later, more professional production done "in the round." I will concede that some plays can be adapted perfectly well to "the round," but *Boardinghouse* is not one of them. Here, certain elements are essential, such as a staircase seen through the french doors and a swinging door to the kitchen. No less critical is a wall in the dining room where Mr. Mumson's portrait can be hung above the sideboard.

I have argued the pros and cons of "theater in the

round" with much better playwrights than myself. Among them, Alan Ayckbourn, who said that I was "hopelessly wedded to the proscenium arch." I don't doubt that he was right.

But, really, what fun would it be to visit a set "in the round" after the last performance? Everything can be seen at a glance from any seat in the house, so why bother?

A novel is another matter. A book has no physical "set," except in the mind of the author (which hopefully will be conveyed through words to the mind of the reader). Therefore, if I want to visit the "set" of my book, I have to travel back in time and memory to the big old house as it existed in the summer of 1943 on the broad, tree-lined street in Sacramento, California.

And so I shall.

My visit begins in the old-fashioned kitchen with its high ceilings, a breakfast nook and a huge black stove where a little girl (myself at the age of eleven) is cooking up one of her strange recipes, as inspired by a serious crank calling herself "Miss Kitchen" in the newspaper. Behind her is a door that opens onto a porch and the splintery steps that lead down to the back yard and the Victory garden. Opposite is the swinging door (always slightly ajar on its rusty hinges), leading to the heart of the house: the dining room.

Pushing open the door, I come to a predictably large (this is a boardinghouse, after all) oak table, with eight mismatched chairs around it. Only seven of the chairs are actually used by the lady I call Mrs. Mumson and her six boarders. The eighth is always left vacant for the late lamented Mr. Mumson, whose portrait hangs above an antique sideboard to the right, just beyond the empty chair. There are depressing wartime blackout curtains at the windows, and a padded window seat with an outlook over the driveway below.

Skirting the table I arrive at the wide, arched doorway that separates the dining room from the parlor. There I can see the usual furniture of the period, a shabby sofa, end tables, and a lamp or two. There are window seats in this room, too, but blackout curtains are missing.

Mentally I retrace my steps, returning to the dining room, the setting of many scenes in the play as well as the novel—from a dreamy dance with Teddy on the Fourth of July to a final, violent confrontation between Teddy and Howard. Off to the left, between the dining room and the parlor, are the three well-worn steps up to the hall where a black candlestick telephone sits on a rickety table next to the staircase. There I see Teddy making a long distance call to the mysterious "Mother Hubbard." I watch once more as he bounds up the stairs in his usual fashion, two at a time, and races down again "like the Exposition Flyer on a downhill grade and three hours behind schedule!"

Of course, the rooms still look like this only in my

mind because, as I have said, the actual house, which in 1943 was a boardinghouse, has undergone a major renovation. (You could say that the owners did the job of "striking" this set when they gutted and remodeled the interior.)

John Steinbeck, in his *Travels with Charlie*, says that Tom Wolfe had it right when he said you can't go home again, because "home" as you knew it only exists in the memory. Seeing places again after a long time can be disturbing. The view seems distorted. What you remembered as a mountain is now a hill. In my own experience, the magnificent Alhambra Theater, with its lush gardens and reflecting pool surrounded by palm trees, had shrunk to half its size when I saw it again twenty years after I danced there.

At the beginning I admitted that I did not know how many of the stories I have often told about the boardinghouse were actually true, and how many were questionable. In that respect, at least, I am in good company. Mark Twain said that he never told the truth without someone thinking it was a lie, and never told a lie without someone thinking it was the truth—and sometimes he didn't know the difference himself!

And so it is with the characters in these pages. That is, they are only *based* on people I knew, simply because I can't recall everything about the real ones. The one character I do recall vividly is Teddy.

Yes, Virginia, there really is a Teddy Soberjowski! (Or was.) And he was just as I have described him: Not particularly tall (barely six feet, I imagined), and not particularly handsome. But, as a young Eileen adds: *Not like a movie star, anyhow. Not like Errol Flynn or Clark Gable. Maybe Sonny Tufts, though.* He did have curly blond hair that fell over his forehead and deep-set blue eyes that sparkled with mischief. Most beguiling of all was his smile. A kind of "killer grin." Like William Holden as a young man, or Jack Nicholson at any age!

The real Teddy Soberjowski had a perplexing and complex character, with personality traits that often seemed in conflict with one another. He could be both tough and gentle, crude and genteel. He was brash and pushy and he rubbed people the wrong way, but didn't give a damn about anyone's opinion (except mine, he said). He knew his way around, that much was obvious. He had grown up on the mean streets of some big city—I've forgotten which one—but I thought there was a hint of New York in his speech.

That was the real Teddy Soberjowski. But was he actually an FBI agent "under cover" at Mrs. Mumson's boardinghouse by day and out nabbing bad guys (and confiscating their expensive cars) by night? I like to think that he was, and who is to say that he was not?

When talking to audiences after a performance of the play, the first thing people want to know is, did I ever see the real Teddy Soberjowski again? The answer is no. Next, did I ever try to get in touch with him, using the card he gave me? Again the answer is no. Then I have to confess that I'm not even sure there ever was such a card. If there was, it got lost somewhere along life's highway. And always there is this question: Have I tried to locate him, using the Internet, for example? Here the answer is yes. But no trace of a Teddy or a Theodore J. Soberjowski has yet been found. I wonder if he even survived the war. A lot of men didn't.

So, what was my fascination with Teddy all about, anyway, and why has it persisted through so many decades? Was I a kid with a crush on an "older man?" (He might have been all of twenty-five when I was eleven.) I remember having a crush on a sixth-grade boy named Raymond Fletcher, the year before. Raymond had a blue bike. Sometimes he would put me on the handlebars and ride me around the block. Naturally, I forgot all about Raymond and his blue bike when Teddy took me for a spin in his red convertible!

A member of the theater audience one night, who claimed to be a clinical psychologist, suggested that Teddy might simply represent all the men in my life that I have loved and lost.

Maybe.

But no matter who or what he was, I will remember Teddy Soberjowski as a tough guy with a kind and compassionate heart, as when he reached out to comfort a little girl who was crying because he was going away. And I recall our last conversation, too, before he rode off into the sunset, when he said, "You'll forget all about me. You'll see!"

But he was wrong about that, wasn't he?